DAUGHTER OF DUST AND THUNDER

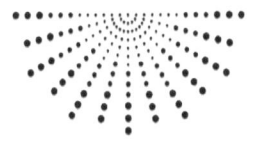

ROBERT G. MUKASA

*To my late mother, **Nobert Nnassaka**, and my late brother, **Andrew Celestine Peter Kamoga.** Your love, strength, and memory continue to light my path.*

CHAPTER ONE

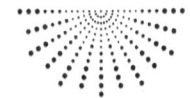

The Nyungu community in Kobole country awoke not by clocks, but by the ancestral rhythm of deep, pulsing, eternal drums. At dawn, the sky blushed in shades of copper and indigo. The earth sighed awake beneath the breath of morning winds. Smoke curled lazily from clay chimneys, mingling with the scent of roasting maize, damp thatch, and the faint musk of red earth freshly kissed by dew. In the fields, women moved like whispers between millet stalks, their bronze skin aglow in the golden light, their ankles jingling with seed-based bangles. Their laughter, soft and bright, floated over the ridges like wind-borne pollen, twining with birdsong and the distant echo of drums rising from the village square.

That morning, the baobabs yawned and stretched their giant limbs toward the rising sun. Spider webs shimmered like silver lace between their roots, beaded with dew. Inside a clay-walled hut, smoothened by generations of hands, a storm broke, not of rain, but of life. Ola entered the world with a defiant howl, her cry raw and fierce, slicing through dawn like lightning. She was not quiet. She did not coo. She thundered.

Ayami Maria, her mother, pressed the newborn to her chest, her breath still ragged, her skin warm and sleek. Her song rose, low and melodic, an ancient lullaby whispered into the morning, its notes curling through the thick, smoky air like threads of incense. The scent of crushed lavender, hibiscus, and shea mingled with blood and clay, filling the air. It was a sacred perfume marking the space between pain and miracle.

Outside, Chief Odu stood tall in the doorway, a lion pelt draped over one shoulder, beads clinking softly across his broad chest. The morning light crowned his graying temples with gold. He did not speak. He only listened to the maternity rites unfolding inside. The child's cry reverberated through the village like a drumbeat of prophecy. He closed his eyes briefly and let the sound wash over him.

"Another child," he thought, his voice rumbling low beneath his breath. "At last, a girl . . . but not just any girl." His gaze fell on the trembling hearth flame and then back to the bundle in Ayami's arms. "This one is born not with a whimper, but with thunder in her throat."

As the drums of Nyungu quickened in the distance, smoke rose into the cobalt sky, and the land itself seemed to lean in and listen. The elders whispered among themselves.

"This girl . . . she does not belong to dust alone. She belongs to thunder."

The Nyungu, where Ola was born, held tightly to the old ways, like roots clinging to the red Kobole soil. Strangers rarely crossed the sacred boundary trees without encountering resistance. Foreigners seldom ventured this deep. And when they did, they were met with polite silence and eyes that said, "*We've seen your kind before, and no, we're not impressed.*" Yet the missionaries came anyway, wearing worn sandals, carrying books of miracles, and smelling of soap. They preached salvation with bread and shame, insisting that one must be clothed to receive the Holy Communion.

This notion did not sit well with the Nyungu. Technically, they knew how to make clothes. The backcloth was there, soft and entirely wearable. But they long held a belief that dressing up was, in some way, an offense to the god of creation, who had chosen to bring them into the world naked. To cover up that divine choice? That would be blasphemy.

Moreover, Nyungu men had their own philosophy: certain parts of the male anatomy, they believed, were meant to swing freely and joyfully in the open air. To the more traditional among them, trousers weren't merely uncomfortable; they were a man-made insult, a quiet rebellion against the creator's original blueprint. Still, Holy Communion came with a dress code.

So, the men of Nyungu devised a workaround that could only be described as holy absurdity. Every Sunday, a single pair of khaki shorts, yes, just one, made the rounds behind the chapel like a sacred relic. That pair of shorts passed from hip to hip, man to man, as they filed before the altar, each receiving the Eucharist with a bowed head and a naked body waiting in the wings of tradition. Nude but not naïve, they stepped forward in solemn defiance.

Ayami Maria chose to baptize her daughter in this chapel thick with cultural drama. So, when Ola turned six, Ayami bathed her skin with water, braided beads into her hair, and led her to a chapel built from mud and stubborn hope. "Your name is Paola now," the Italian priest said as he sprinkled the holy water on the girl's brow, sealing the baptism with a foreign name.

That day, Chief Odu, Ola's father, stood at the edge of the grass-thatched church like a goat sniffing unfamiliar herbs: curious but unconvinced. Inside, the preacher bellowed about salvation and sanctification, but Odu's mind was busy with more pressing calculations, namely, how many of his eight wives could sit in the pews without provoking a holy scandal. One-husband-one-wife? That sounded less like divine wisdom and more like famine. He scratched his head. How could a God who supposedly turned water into wine not understand a man's need for options?

Then there was the matter of eating Christ's body. The missionary had said it with trembling reverence, but all Odu heard was cannibalism. Under the mango tree, he whispered to his cousin, "So, we must now chew the bones of their prophet to be saved?" His cousin nearly choked on the communion wafer, torn between horror and the risk of laughing his way to hellfire. He was unsure if laughing in church meant instant hellfire.

And the story of Maria, the Jewish virgin mother, was pure comedy. Odu had watched Reverend Tobi, the poor, sweating Italian soul, trying to explain it to a circle of bare-breasted Nyungu women sprawled on the grass, as if they were waiting for moonlight gossip. "She was . . . untouched," he stammered, hands fluttering like lost birds.

One elder woman leaned forward, breasts swinging like pendulums of disbelief, and asked, "By no one?" The silence was so thick you could slice it with a calabash, until it burst into laughter: raw, generous, and uncountable. Tobi's face flushed redder than palm wine. He abandoned the topic entirely, retreating to talking about Moses and the burning bush. But the greatest betrayal, in Odu's view, was arithmetic.

Back in fireside school, he had learned with absolute certainty that one plus one plus one made three. A truth as solid as a chief's ego. Yet here were the missionaries, robed in authority, claiming that one plus one plus one somehow equaled . . . one, the Trinity. Divine mathematics, they called it. Odu called it Western confusion disguised in holy robes.

So, he straddled two worlds like a reluctant acrobat: one foot planted in the drum-beating, ancestor-honoring faith of his fathers, the other twitching uneasily inside the smoke-filled, hymn-humming chambers of foreign salvation. He was willing to learn, but to trade logic for a ghost who returned after three days just because some preacher said so. After all, even the village goat, if resurrected, would be marched straight to the healer for questioning. And so, Odu watched half-amused, half-puzzled, as Ayami believed.

Staying home with his eight wives, Chief Odu sat beneath the shade of his thatched palace, fingers wrapped around a pipe, muttering about men who had risen from the dead. He often scoffed at the white man's arithmetic. "Three persons in one God?" he would grumble, shaking his head. "Then my herd of goats must all be one goat, too." Odu had yet to chew through the gristle of Christian logic. He believed in gods who whispered through baobab trees, not in stories of virgins giving birth to sons or corpses walking again. Still, he never forbade his household from embracing Christianity. He let faith brush against their lives like wind gently brushing the grass without uprooting it. Ayami believed he watched.

This Odu, son of Ode, had not been baptized but wore the title of Chief with unmistakable pride. The day he ascended to leadership still lingers in whispers among Nyungu elders. His father's burial had gathered all his sons into the Nyungu forest, where carved stools formed a crescent beneath the watchful gaze of every circumcised man. Seven sons sat naked on those stools, their manhood dangling low. The ritual was clear: he whose male pride touched the earth would inherit the chiefdom. Laughter came only in hindsight; in that moment, the air was thick with solemnity and ancestral judgment. When Odu's male endowment brushed the soil, the elders cheered, rose, and declared him the heir. From that day, his words carried the force of law.

Odu wore the Chief's authority like a second skin. His compound bloomed with wives, one daughter, and many sons. His granaries bulged with tribute. He ruled with nine wives, high fertility rates, and extensive livestock holdings.

Among his children, none outshone Ola. When she walked, it was more gliding than stepping, her feet barely kissing the dust, her hips swaying like tall reeds in a breeze. The daughter of Odu knew she was beautiful and wielded that beauty with quiet confidence. When boys crossed her path, she did not step aside; she twirled. Her laughter, flung like music over her shoulder, wrapped around their hearts like creeping vines. Men forgot what they were discussing when she walked through the village. For her movement was not mere motion; it was melody. Her almond-shaped eyes, alight with mischief, could melt even Odu's most stoic resolve. The

Chief, who spoke to his wives with the firmness of command, softened when she looked up at him. Her voice dipped into a coaxing tone that turned his 'no' into 'yes' with a single blink.

Yet, despite her beauty, Ola hated the word "woman". To her, it clung to weakness. To be a woman in Nyungu was to hold your tongue and nod. Speak too boldly, and you'd be reminded, "don't be a woman." Village meetings took place under the sacred tree, but no woman ever sat there. Instead, they simmered in kitchens, eyes gleaming with untold stories. Even when wronged, a woman's voice had to pass through her husband's mouth, and heaven help her if he was the one who caused the harm.

One day, an elder barked at a boy, "Don't be a woman!" Ola, grinding millet beside her mother, froze. Her hands tightened around the grinding stone, and thunder gathered behind her eyes.

To peek further into her bag of fury: once, when her brother mocked her for not being able to pee while standing, she hurled a pestle at him. The paste missed, but the message landed squarely. This girl, who could hush birds with her singing, also had a punch capable of realigning a brother's jaw. Her temper was wildfire: inherited and easily stoked. Ayami, too, could boil over with the slightest spark. And Odu? His fury had once chased a trader out of the homestead for asking the price of a cow twice.

Strangely, Ola's beauty only made her fire more enchanting. She could curse and captivate in the same breath.

At thirteen, when the first elder whispered, "That one will make a fine wife," Ola spat into the fire.

"Let him try to carry me," she muttered, loud enough to cause unease. "He will limp forever."

Her mother scolded her in hushed tones, but Ola's voice rose like wind before a storm. "I was not born to decorate another man's hut," she said. "I was not shaped by thunder just to fetch his bathwater."

By the time she was fourteen, men had stopped calling her beautiful. They called her wild. Rebellious. Dangerous.

"She'll break a man's spirit," one muttered.

"She'll curse the cows," said another.

But they still watched.

They watched her run with her brothers, wrestling them into the dust, climbing trees, and daring snakes to blink. She was stronger than most boys her age. And yet, amid all that heat and defiance, she still hummed to herself when alone, her voice sweet enough to hush birds' mid-song. Her songs were both lullabies and war cries.

In Ayami's hut, she did everything: pounding, sweeping, and weaving. Never once asking what belonged to which gender. Her brothers joked that the only thing she had not mastered was aiming her urine at trees. Still, none of them dared to challenge her in a fight. Because when Ola swung, someone bled.

At sixteen, she was both storm and song, a mirror of her mother's youthful fire, tempered by the boldness of the boys she called kin. Her body danced between traditions, curved like a goddess, yet built to fight like a brother. Even her father, the unflinching patriarch, often stared at her in awe, wondering how such power could be encased in such beauty.

At night, Odu sat in the doorway of his compound,

watching his daughter from afar. "Mamu," he whispered, invoking the goddess of beauty and fertility, "you outdid yourself." He pictured the cows that would soon line up at his gate, each a dowry offering. His grin spread wide in the moonlight.

Ola grew up among goats and grounds, with the scent of roasted maize and red dust in the air. Her skin was silk-smooth, her laughter like wind chimes, and she held her father's favor like a charm. However, what she longed for most was something she would never have. As she watched her brothers strut past, that small external token of masculinity became a symbol of all she could never claim to be. She would often stare into the river's reflection and murmur, "If only I had been born with one." Despite this private ache, Nyungu's past and future collided with Ola, a radiant, unruly, and defiant force.

One morning, her bare toes curled into the dew-wet earth as she crouched behind a reed fence to eavesdrop. Inside her father's hut, deep voices pulsed against the mud walls. Strange, clipped syllables tangled with the gravel growl of Chief Odu.

That morning, the missionaries arrived with books in hand and crosses around their necks. Their robes were stiff with starch, and their skin shone. They spoke of reading, writing, futures stitched in ink, and learning. Chief Odu spat thick phlegm into the fire, his gaze as hard as dried cowhide.

"No daughter of mine," he growled, "will carry chalk instead of a calabash."

The air inside was thick with smoke and sweat. The scent of burning shea butter clung to the thatch, but Ola barely noticed. Her heart throbbed in her throat as she pressed her ear to the gap in the wall.

Aya's voice sliced through the haze like cool water, pleading, soft, but fierce. "She has the eyes of a seeker, Odu. Let her try."

Outside, Ola's hands gripped the reeds more tightly. Her pulse raced with something she had never named before: hope.

Chief Odu stood. His voice thundered. "A woman belongs in the smoke of the kitchen, not under the gaze of a stranger's god!"

The argument cracked like lightning. Aya's silence afterward was more devastating than the storm. After the Chief's refusal, the missionaries departed in a trial of dust and disappointment. One of them carried a tattered Bible, its gold-rimmed pages fluttering in the breeze like the wings of a bird. Something about it beckoned Ola. As they left, their boots left strange, neat tracks in the compound. She traced them with her finger long after they were gone.

That night, as the crickets sang and the moon cast silver across the compound, Ola lay awake. Her fingers danced across the dirt floor, sketching letters she had never been taught. Her eyes burned with questions she could not yet ask.

In some far-off chamber of her heart, school began to taste like freedom: bitter with defiance, sharp with yearning, and sweet like something just out of reach.

A week passed. Then another. The dust from the missionaries' departure had long settled, but not in Ola's spirit. Each morning, she rose before the rooster's cry, sweeping the compound with quiet fury. She no longer hummed while peeling cassava or fetching water. Instead, she stared into the fire with eyes too old for her fourteen years, her lips drawn tight, her joy dimmed.

Aya watched her daughter begin to fold into herself, like a

leaf in drought. When Ola started pressing charcoal onto stones to mimic writing, Aya's chest ached with quiet pride but with silence. She tried again to plead with Odu, this time not with words but with silence. She stopped singing in the kitchen. Ayami let pots clash a little louder. Aya's behavior did not escape Chief Odu's innately watchful eye.

One evening, as the sun sank behind the hills and bathed the homestead in soft copper light, Chief Odu sat beneath the talking tree, plucking feathers from a guinea fowl. The scent of smoked herbs clung to his wrapper. His gourd of millet beer sat untouched. From the corner of his eye, he saw her, Ola, the apple of his eye, perched by the fire, shaping ash into the curves of letters she had never seen. Her fingers moved as if remembering something from another life.

He grunted, but she did not flinch.

"Do you know the name of what you're drawing?" he barked.

She paused and met his gaze

"Not yet," she replied.

A long silence stretched between them, thick with pride and sorrow too ancient to name. Odu chewed his lip, his thoughts tangled like the roots of the old baobab. She was his only daughter. To let her go into the hands of foreign gods, to lose her to ink and chalk, felt like setting his own breath on fire.

But then again, wasn't she already burning?

He spat into the dust and stood.

"You will go," he said gruffly. "But the first time I hear you have disrespected your mother's mortar or forgotten the smell of this earth, I will drag you back by your ears."

Ola stared, not quite believing it, her body still as a statue.

Then she sprang like a calf released from a tether, her arms flung around his waist, her laughter breaking through like thunder in a dry season.

That night, she danced by the fire until her feet blistered. Aya, her mother sang again. Odu pretended not to smile, sipped his beer, and muttered, "Let them teach her their letters. She is still Nyungu blood."

The morning Chief Odu took Ola to school, the sun had not yet fully climbed the sky. A hush lay over the land, broken only by the cooing of doves and the mowing of cattle. Dew clung to the blades of elephant grass like tears refusing to fall. Ola walked beside her father in silence, her heart drumming faster than her feet. The village soil, still cool and damp, clung to her soles, and her fingers itched to hold something, perhaps a pencil or maybe just the future.

Odu walked tall, his broad back glistening with sweat and his stride slow but unwavering. He wore only a faded leopard-print loincloth tied loosely around his waist; the rest of his body was bare to the wind. His staff tapped the earth with each step, steady and rhythmic, like an elder's clock. The Chief smelled of shea butter, smoke, and strength.

The school building had barely cured bricks, a tin roof that blinked in the sunlight, and a chalkboard that hung like a shrine, sat at the edge of the bush like a foreign object. Birds chattered noisily from a nearby fig tree, and the wind carried a sharp, unfamiliar scent; part ink, part starch, and something entirely foreign.

Inside, children sat stiffly on wooden stools, scratching letters onto slates with chalk that squeaked like crying termites. At the front stood Miss Rosa, a small, pale Italian woman in a stiff blue dress and thick-soled shoes that made no sound when she walked. Her scent filled the room, medicinal and sour, like crushed lemon leaves.

When Odu entered, the room fell silent. His height darkened the doorway. He ducked to enter, his beads clinking softly, and strode to the front like a chief inspecting his warriors. He lowered himself onto a stool far too small for his frame. The wood creaked under his weight. In the process of sitting, his loincloth shifted, revealing his contest-winning manhood to the open air, like an uninvited guest.

Gasps fluttered across the room. A girl squealed. A boy dropped his slate. Miss Rosa's eyes widened, and her pink face turned a shocking red. Her hands flew to her mouth and then to her rosary. "*Oh, Dio mio,*" she whispered, crimson and horrified. Her gaze darted everywhere but Odu's lap.

But Odu sat proud, arms crossed, expression unmoved, like a mountain sculpted by time. He spoke with the calm of smoldering firewood: "This is my daughter. Her name is Ola. Teach her what you think is important. But she will return home each evening to pound yams and remember whose daughter she is."

He stood and he left.

Miss Rosa nodded rigidly, mechanically, as if her neck was carved from soapstone.

Ola, her cheeks hot with both shame and a laughter she dared not release, took a seat on the back bench. The chalk felt strange in her hand, cold, dry, and full of promise. She traced the first letter of her name, O, like a drum, her mouth wide in awe.

The words came slowly at first. But soon the sound on the board, *ah, beh, keh,* stretched out like songs in her throat. The classroom smelled of dust, sweat, and the promise of fresh beginnings. Sunlight poured through the holes in the roof, striping the floor like a zebra's back.

By midday, she was humming again. And though her father's bare presence still lingered like a ghost in everyone's minds, the lesson went on. That evening, as she walked back home, her fingers were dusted white with chalk. Her mouth was buzzing with strange new words, and her spirit swelled so full, it nearly spilled from her chest.

CHAPTER TWO

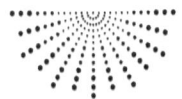

"Olaaaaa! Ola, daughter of Odu, granddaughter of Ode! How many times must I call you? Get out of bed. It is time for school." Aya's voice pierced the still morning, shattering the cold silence. It curled through the thatched roof and sliced into Ola's dreams like the circumcision blade she feared. The chill hung heavily in the air, thick as fog, creeping beneath the mat on the bamboo bed where Ola lay curled like a question mark. Her limbs drew tight under the warmth of the thick raffia blanket. The morning bit at her toes when she dared slip one out. She quickly yanked it back in. Maybe, just maybe, her mother's voice would melt into the wind if she remained still. But Aya's voice was steel wrapped in silk, beautiful, firm, and laced with warmth. There was danger in every vowel. Ola tested the cold again with a tentative foot and quickly withdrew. This time, however, her mother's tone offered no room for delay. The raffia blanket flew off the bamboo bed, her heart thudding. Ola leapt from the warmth, her bare feet slapping against the earthen floor; the nightgown, given to her by Miss Rosa, clung to her skin.

She knelt by the bamboo bedframe and whispered her morning prayers with hurried reverence. Her mother believed this ritual was sacred. Her father, Chief Odu, dismissed it as a waste of time. But in her mother's hut, the rules were not up for debate. Ayami would not tolerate a daughter who skipped God, especially on a day such as that one.

Outside, the *Pom-Pom* rumbled across the village like distant thunder. The Nyungu traditional drum's rhythm was neither mournful nor warlike. It was bright, high-pitched, pulsing with celebration and song. Women's voices danced through the air, woven with ululations and the soft slap of bare feet on earth. Ola's stomach twisted. She recognized the tune before she could name it. The annual circumcision season had arrived, summoned by the jubilant chorus of village women. This time, the melody carried her name. She reluctantly stepped outside.

Women crowded the village paths, singing and ululating, their voices braided in joyful harmony. Ola's stomach clenched. Her mother's hut buzzed with energy, giggling voices, bustling hands, women arriving with baskets of this and that, and whispers of delight. Preparations began in earnest. As the Chief's daughter, her royal name passed from lip to lip like a blessing. Everyone smiled when they spoke of it. But her own smile never quite reached her eyes.

The circumcision season had returned. The thought sliced through her like a knife. Ola stood frozen as the truth settled in. She was sixteen. This year, she was one of them. As tradition dictated, under the full August moon, the village gathered girls her age. Their skin shone with palm oil, their bodies adorned, and their heads held high, only because they were told to. Then they would sing, dance, and circle the village endlessly until their legs trembled. Then came the forest.

In the shade of ancient trees, older women, whose hands shook yet were sure where to cut, taught the girls, who were ripe for circumcision, for three days and nights. There were no books, only listening and memorizing every word about marriage, obedience, and duty. When exhaustion hollowed out the girls, the cutting would begin.

At noon, with the sun blazing directly overhead, the eldest of the blade-wielding women would call upon Mama, the fertility goddess. The blade then appeared. It did not care that it was wrapped in tradition. It sliced without apology. With their knees trembling, each girl lay down and opened her legs to the old gods. They called it womanhood. No man in Nyungu would marry an uncut girl. To resist the blade was to choose exile or, worse, punishment. Ola had heard of some girls who fled, only to be dragged back.

No medicine. No mercy. Only the gleam of metal and the scent of sorghum. In Nyungu, saying that bacteria caused infection was like claiming to see ghosts in the daylight. Ola had heard of girls who bled for too long. Of mothers who wept over their lifeless daughters, buried in shallow forest graves. Still, the village danced. How could they celebrate? How could mothers sing while their daughters bled? Teacher Rosa's voice echoed in her mind, fabulous, foreign, and fierce; "It's mutilation, not initiation," she had once whispered. "They call it tradition, but it is pain disguised as pride. It is sheer female genital mutilation." Ola believed her. But belief was not a shield against the knife of the ancient Nyungu wizards.

"Olaaaa! Are you now Lot's wife? Shall I fetch a broom to sweep up your salt?" Aya's voice jolted her back to the present. She scrambled into her uniform, fastened her belt, and bolted down the path to Stella Maris School. Her checkered dress flapped behind her like a flag, part banner of education, part shield against what awaited her.

The sky was cloudless, but a storm churned within her. She was late to school. When she entered her class, teacher Avilla paused mid-equation, with the chalk frozen on the board. Ola braced for rebuke. But Avilla's eyes softened, and a silent understanding passed between them. The teacher said nothing. She simply nodded. She knew what awaited Ola the next day, the circumcision knife.

Ola took her seat, opened her notebook, and tried to find solace in the numbers. But the equations blurred. The chalkboard dissolved into mist. Her mind swirled with escape routes, bush paths, hidden tracks, and the impossible choices. Would she run? Could she survive?

During the break, Teacher Avilla, a Nyunguan, beckoned her. Ola's heart sank. "My sister," the teacher whispered. "It's nothing. The older woman goes chop-chop with the knife. Over in a flash." Ola nodded and managed a smile, but inside, she was screaming.

Outside the latrines, another teacher, called Alana, appeared with a solemn face. She had heard of Ola's fate.

"If I were your age, I'd run," she said, her voice cracking. "But we are only women. . . ." The words wrapped themselves around Ola's heart. Her breath caught. No one had ever said it out loud before.

Confused, Ola ran to the staffroom, heart hammering, searching for teacher Rosa, the Italian, the only adult who dared to question the sacred knife. But she was told that Rosa was gone. She had vanished like hope. With her trusted teacher gone without explanation, the day dragged on. Ola didn't eat. She didn't speak. When the school ended, she walked home as if every step pulled her further from the girl she used to be.

By the time she reached home, the music was thundering. Drums and flutes roared. Women wailed joy into the dusk. Her mother stirred a pot, her face radiant with pride. Odu emerged from his *nkwa,* his official hut, with the grin of a man full to the brim with satisfaction. He did not hug her. He could not, not yet. His eyes glowed with unspoken excitement. "Two hundred cows," he thought. "She will be the sixth wife of Chief Kakobe, the eighty-year-old. Kakobe will be pleased. A daughter worthy of legend."

Ola did not know she had already been promised to the old man, Kakobe, as a wife. The deal was done.

Inside her hut, the fire roared. She stripped off her uniform and tied her loincloth around her waist. For once, it felt foreign on her skin. Her thoughts spiraled. Outside, she heard women preparing for her future. Inside, the girl on the bamboo bed bit her lip to silence her sobs. She stared at the ceiling. Tears slipped down her cheek. Could she run? Could she betray them all? Tomorrow, after circumcision, she would no longer be a child, unless she ran away from home.

That night, supper tasted like sand. The council's

messenger had arrived, rituals already discussed, and everyone had slept early in view of the events of the following day.

CHAPTER THREE

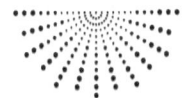

The night clung to the village like a shroud. Inside the hut, Ola lay motionless, her eyes wide open, ears straining for the faintest hint of movement. The rhythm of her breath was the only thing she dared to control. Around her, her brothers slept like logs, except for Nunu, whose snores rose and fell like waves. The low-pitched rumble grated on her nerves but comforted her all the same. It meant he was deeply asleep. It meant she had time. In her mind, she had crafted a plan. Vanishing from Nyungu was it!

Tradition dictated that, since Ola was due for circumcision, her mother, Aya, would attend to her father's needs that night, leaving Ola unobserved. Aya's absence was another window of opportunity.

After midnight, her fingers trembled as she slid off the bamboo bed. Her heart was not beating; it was battering her chest like a war drum. Every breath sounded loud. When she reached for the blue school uniform dangling from a crooked stick on the wall, it slipped from her fingers and hit the floor with a thud, like thunder. She froze, every cell in her body listening. Nunu stirred. Mumbled. A sound like her name fumbled from his sleep-drunk mouth. She held her breath until his snoring resumed.

She crept toward the bamboo door, fingers curling around its edge. As she lifted it, it groaned in protest with a long, raspy swish. Nunu shifted again and muttered nonsense. Ola's grip turned sweaty. She lowered the door slowly and carefully, as if returning a scalding coal. Only when the night reclaimed its silence did she venture out.

The courtyard yawned before her, cloaked in darkness. Trees stood like ancient sentinels, twisted arms outstretched, their shadows long and monstrous. The air was cool and nearly wet. Goosebumps prickled her skin.

The darkness was thick. The trees cast ghostly silhouettes. A chill ran up her spine, a rustle. Something furry brushed against her leg. Her stomach dropped. She leaped back, fists clenched over her mouth, fighting the scream that clawed its way up her throat. It was a rat.

Then, "Who goes there?"

Her father's voice. Loud, sharp, and threatening.

She froze mid-breath.

A pause. Silence stretched taut. A mattress creaked inside his hut. After a moment, he muttered something about stray dogs. Then nothing. No footsteps. No rustling spear. No angry grunt. The gods had bought her seconds. Only when his snores returned and her eyes adjusted did she creep past her father's *nkwa.* The central hut loomed like a watchtower, flanked by a semicircle of his wives' huts. The design of the homestead seemed built to guard against escape.

But she was already past the compound, into the brush.

Her feet pounded the earth in a steady rhythm, fear her only fuel. The world around her rustled, chirped, and growled as she pressed on. Every whisper of the forest reminded her of the blade, the gleaming metal that awaited her at dawn. The knife that carved girls into women, in Nyungu's eyes. But for Ola, it meant only pain.

By sunrise, she had covered several miles. Her body ached, but her will burned hotter than ever. She had one destination: the missionaries' parish. The priests had machines, motorcycles, and cars to reach the scattered outposts of the mission. But girls like her had only legs, fear, and desperation.

In the heavy silence of the morning, her thoughts wandered. Faces of girls she knew rose like ghosts: Avim, who married a toothless man at sixteen because her father saw cows in her smile. A man who could not pronounce her name without swallowing it whole, he called her Afwim instead of Avim, thanks to his missing front teeth. He couldn't even whistle.

Love had no place in Nyungu's customs. Girls were inherited like clay pots. A brother or son, anyone but the mother, could claim the widow when the father died. This was called protection. She remembered Teacher Rosa's lessons about the spread of chronic diseases through such customs. But the Nyungu did not believe in diseases they couldn't see.

She thought of *Kolobi,* which sealed a girl's fate. Kolobi was a Nyungu custom where circumcised boys chased virgin girls for marriage. The faster the virgin, the better for her. In the Nyungu community, circumcised boys hunted girls randomly. The girls were expected to run. If caught, they would twist their legs like vines, resisting the fall, resisting fate. But if the girl liked the boy, her resistance melted into the marriage ritual. This is how her mother, Aya, became Odu's wife. She had chosen her hunter long before the hunt.

But Ola had not chosen. She would not be caught.

By mid-morning, her legs felt like firebrands. Her steps faltered. She pushed deeper into the thicket, brushing past thorny shrubs until the world narrowed to a cocoon of dry leaves. Her body collapsed. She barely managed to curl up before sleep swallowed her.

She dreamed of old women with rotting breath and blood-filled nails chasing her through a forest of skulls. Their knives flashed. Their cackles rang hollow. One lunged, their teeth bared like tusks. Ola screamed awake, her heart racing. Sweat slicked her back. Her limbs had turned into jelly. She tried to stand but failed. She was starving. Hunger was now an ache, deep and gnawing, like termites chewing her bones.

The thought of home returned uninvited. Her brothers' faces. Her mother's eyes. Her father's fury. Would she be punished? Speared? Or welcomed back with open arms and a blade?

Then came the rain. The sky cracked open and hurled down stones of ice. Hail pelted the earth. She crouched in the thicket, her skin numb, clothes soaked through. Her body trembled violently, a leaf-matted ghost of the girl who had fled the Chief's hut. She huddled there, shivering as the storm raged like the turmoil within her.

As twilight draped its veil over the land, she began to stir. Every step was a battle. Her soul floated. Her body stumbled. She moved like a shadow, driven by the barest thread of will. By midnight, she staggered through the gates of the catholic parish and collapsed on its lawn. Barking erupted. Growls followed. Then the sound of footsteps. Lanterns flared.

Father Angelo appeared in his long johns, hair tousled, chest heaving. He parted the gathering with an urgency born of faith and instinct. Kneeling beside her, he touched her wrist.

She was still alive. But barely.

He lifted her with care, as if handling something sacred, and laid her on a couch. He vanished briefly, then returned with a black case marked with a red cross. He worked in silence, pressing here, tilting there while whispering soft words.

She coughed, gasped, then opened her eyes. A green public cup was placed in her trembling hands. She drank, guzzled, as if it were holy water. Then food. Warm. Sweet. Ambrosial. She ate like someone trying to swallow their pain. When she had finished eating, the priest knelt beside her.

"What happened, child?"

Her lips trembled, but she spoke. The story poured out thick, jagged, raw, a torrent of tradition, terror, and torn choices. Father Angelo listened in silence. His face drained of colour. His knuckles whitened. The horror crept over him like frost. When her voice finally broke, he gently covered her with a blanket and placed a pillow beneath her head. She closed her eyes. For the first time in days, she slept without fear. The priest sat in half-dark, watching her breathe.

"What next?" he whispered into the silence. It was a question that haunted him long after dawn. Returning her to her father, Chief Odu, could mean death. However, by harboring her, he risked angering the powerful Chief. Father Angelo sat still, caught between duty and compassion, searching for a path through the storm.

CHAPTER FOUR

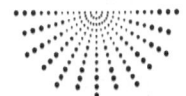

O n the fifth day, Ola's strength returned with vengeance. Once drained and pale, her skin now shimmered under the sun, a defiant glow that turned heads and stirred whispers. The circumcised women narrowed their eyes and silently cursed behind their stiff smiles. Yet none dared to voice their disdain. She was royalty. Her presence carried weight, her gaze was sharper than any blade.

When Father Angelo drew her into conversation, her mind sparked like flint. Insight flashed from her lips with such precision that even the priest, seasoned, celibate, and sworn to God, felt his heart pound a dangerous rhythm.

"She once asked me," he would later recall, "If your God is just, why do His sons bleed us to keep their tradition?"

With every hour she spent at the parish, the coil in Angelo's chest twisted tighter. She was brilliance and rebellion wrapped in flesh, a walking spark in a dry forest. He prayed for courage, clasped the rosary until his fingers numbed, and then, one dawn, slid into the driver's seat of his rusted Fiat to confront the mighty Odu, Chief of the Nyungu.

The Fiat screamed to life like a tortured soul, *Nkwankwankwa! Nkwankwankwa!* The villagers had named it for the sound it made, a badge of ridicule and a legend. Its coughing engine roared into the misty morning, warning the world that the priest of the white gods was on the move.

He gripped the wheel with white knuckles, his nerves fraying as he drove straight into rebel territory. The New Freedom Pact (NFP) lurked in those woods, ghosts with guns, desperate, angry youths who slit a man's throat for a loaf of bread or the metal in his rings. He glanced at the crucifix on his dashboard and whispered a prayer, "Santa Maria, keep me invisible."

The road buckled beneath him. Steam hissed from the radiator, forcing him to stop and feed the dying machine with bottle after bottle of lukewarm water. As he fidgeted, sweat poured down his neck. Each moment was a roll of the dice with death.

By mid-afternoon, he crested the hill at Nyungu. A dusty crowd awaited. Children ran beside the vehicle, chanting its name in gleeful chaos. *"Nkwankwankwa! Nkwankwankwa!"* The Fiat shuddered and wheezed as if embarrassed.

Angelo barely stepped out before sweets vanished into tiny palms and laughter floated like smoke. But beneath the smiles, tension twisted through the air like a coiled wire.

Aya Maria, the Chief's first wife, stood at the entrance, her hands in reverence and dread. "I see you, my Father."

"I see you, my daughter," Angelo replied, forcing a smile, though his bones ached with apprehension.

Inside the compound, the warmth vanished. The huts stood slow and wide, their mud walls cracked with age, smoke spiraling from soot-blackened roofs. The men's eyes burned with suspicion. The women's chatter broke off at his footsteps. The priest was offered a three-legged stool on which he sat stiff and guarded. Aya vanished into the Chief's *Nkwa*. The others shared sweets, their final act of peace before the war.

Then Odu emerged, tall and bare-chested. His eyes were stormy, ancient, and unmoved.

"I see you, lion of Nyungu," Angelo said, his voice even.

Odu studied him. "Is it raining where you came from?"

"No rain. Only news about the New Freedom Pact rebels. Only madness."

The Chief nodded calmly like a coiled thunder. "They will learn. When a mosquito lands on a man's testicle, he knows violence is not the only answer."

Angelo exhaled slowly, and a flicker of relief crossed his face. "Then perhaps we speak now, not in fists, but in truth."

"Speak," Odu commanded.

"I come not for myself, but for justice. Your daughter, Ola, escaped a death that she did not deserve. Her blood may be Nyungu, but her mind has seen the light of the world. Knowledge is her armor. You may not know it, but circumcision is a blade that cuts more than just flesh. It severs futures. She is alive, Chief. Safe. But she ran from torture, not tradition."

Silence fell like a blade.

Then . . . *thunder*.

"Foolish dog!" Odu roared. "You came here to spit on my gods? To twist my daughter's mind with your white lies?"

He turned to his wife, his eyes ablaze. "This is your doing! You bore me a disgrace!"

His palm cracked against her cheek, sharp and loud as a whip.

Nunu, Ola's brother, lunged forward, angry and foolish, to defend his mother. The Chief's fist found his ribs. The boy dropped like a broken branch.

Angelo shot up in panic but froze. Odu's glare pinned him like a spear.

"I should tear you limb from limb," the Chief growled. "But I remember we tried that once with a white man. He came back in the belly of iron ships."

The air thickened. Even the trees seemed to hold their breath.

"Listen well," Odu said, voice low and lethal. "You and your kind, who always want to be the bride at every wedding and the corpse at every funeral, you will leave. In two days. Take your God and your lies and disappear. This is our land, not your Christ's. My daughter will be dragged back and face the gods. Dead or alive."

He barked orders. Drums answered. Warriors stirred. A village bristled. Panic licked the walls like fire on dry thatch. Some people whispered that Ola was pregnant. Others said that it was worse; she had become a nun. Aya's wails pierced the air. Other women joined, keening like the wind before a storm. The courtyard buckled into chaos.

Angelo slipped away.

Into the Fiat. Into gear. Onto the road.

"Faster, you cursed thing! I must warn Ola," he shouted, the old car groaning beneath him.

Back in the square, Odu raised his voice.

"Nyungu omu . . . !"

"Oleeeee!" the warriors thundered back.

"She has stabbed our honor and desecrated our gods!" Odu bellowed. "Bring her back. Alive or not."

Spears gleamed. Shields rattled. Feet pounded the earth.

Okeke led them. He was an iron-fisted, silent killer. He needed no words to instill fear; his silence alone was enough to do the work. It hung heavier than war drums, echoed like an ancestral curse, and cut sharper than the gods' own blades. Where others bared teeth or shouted threats, he stared, cold, measured, unblinking, and men stepped aside. Blood never touched him by accident; every mark was deliberate. Every blow, precise. Even in stillness, he seemed coiled like a viper, waiting, not from doubt, but with certainty. He always struck at the exact moment his prey had given up hope.

This silent killer did not kill in anger. He killed with clarity. Each death under his hand was calculated, executed as if dictated by a code only he could hear. His silence was not empty; it was honed, intentionally sharpened to the edge of a blade. Under his command, danger itself took form. Under his command, the Nyungu warriors moved like ghosts through the forest shortcuts, unseen and unheard. No lights guided their way. No whispers passed between them. They breathed in perfect rhythm, bound to a singular purpose that Okeke had etched deep into their hearts: bring her back to face the gods.

Meanwhile, Angelo raced through the darkness. The Fiat coughed, spat, and died.

"No. No!" he pleaded, throwing the door open and

wrenching the hood up. He slammed his palms against the engine. "You stubborn mule of a machine!"

Sweat trickled down his back as he emptied the last of his water into the engine. The forest closed in, silent, watchful.

Then, shadows. Two men emerged from the darkness. Guns raised. Faces unreadable.

"Identify yourself," one hissed.

Angelo's breath vanished. "I . . . I'm a priest."

A flash of movement. The rifle butt cracked against the priest's temple. He staggered, collapsing to his knees, his blood trailing into the dust.

The rebels said nothing. They ransacked the Fiat. They found gold, an Italian wireless set, and a first-aid kit. Their grins gleamed like blades beneath the moonlight.

CHAPTER FIVE

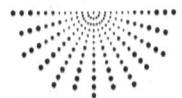

T ruth be told, Odu's blow cracked across Nunu's face like
lightning splitting a tree. It was sharp, hot, and disorient-
ing. Stars danced in his vision. Blood rushed to his ears,
muffling the chaos around him. But he could not afford to
stumble, not now. His sister's life dangled on the cliffs of fate.

He staggered backward, lip split, the coppery taste of blood
spreading in his mouth. His legs quivered beneath him, but he
did not fall. He locked eyes with the man who had struck him,
Odu, his father, a towering storm of wrath in a warrior's regalia.
Yet behind the fury, Nunu glimpsed something else in Odu's
gaze. Hesitation and fear, not for Nunu, but for Aya, his
mother. Odu would not dare to cross her line again. She could
defend herself.

But Ola could not. Without another glance, Nunu turned
and limped away, weaving through shouting relatives, overturned
stools, and clattering spears. At the back of the homestead, now a
brewing war front, he crouched beside the *nkwa*, gasping like a

wounded antelope. He wiped the blood from his nose using the back of his hand. No one noticed him. All eyes and ears were on the confrontation between Odu and the stunned priest.

The moment was ripe. He slipped unnoticed into the thickets. Adrenaline surged through his veins, washing away the dizziness. His father's blow still stung, but his resolve burned hotter. He rose like a charging bull, his usual trot erupting into a sprint. The wind lashed his cheeks. The earth thudded beneath his bare feet. Each breath was a silent prayer. Each step a promise.

Ola's face danced in his mind, wide-eyed, hopeful, fragile. Behind her, Okeke's sneering face loomed, snarling like a hyena. That vision made him faster.

Night fell around him like a hunter's net, thick, black, and enclosing. Hyenas whooped in the distance, but Nunu ran on. The bush clawed at his legs. Insects swarmed his ears. Still, he did not slow. The road to the parish twisted like a serpent, but he knew its curves. He also knew Odu's army would take time to recover from the shock. Tradition dragged its feet.

At last, he reached the parish's edge, his chest heaving and legs trembling. He did not approach the gate. Instead, he crouched behind the hedgerow, cupped his hands, and made a raven's cry soft and rhythmic. It was their childhood signal.

A pause. Then the same sound, hesitant.

"Ola," he whispered. "It's me."

Footsteps. Shadows. Then she appeared. Her eyes locked on him. Her mouth opened, but no words came. They collided in each other's arms, two halves of the same soul. Her tears soaked into his shoulder. His hands trembled on her back.

When they sat on the verandah, Nunu's eyes darted everywhere, skittish and alert. Ola touched his arm.

"What is it?" she asked, voice low.

"You left me," he said, the pain cracking his voice. "You just ran. I thought I was your favorite brother."

She held his gaze, fierce and sorrowful. "I left to protect you. You're alive because I didn't tell you."

"Alive, yes, but for how long?" he fired back. "They're coming for you, Ola. Our father unleashed the Nyungu warriors. We have to go. Now."

Shock washed over her face. "Mother? Father Angelo?"

He grabbed her wrist. "Mother is suffering. Father Angelo. . . ." He looked away. "He might already be dead."

Her breath caught. "No."

"I came to take you away," Nunu said emphatically. "We run. Tonight."

But Ola shook her head. "I am not dragging you into this. I've hurt too many already."

"You'll hurt me more if you stay," he said, his voice cracking. "If they find me, I'm dead too. So, you go with me, or no one goes."

She stared at him, torn, then nodded.

Behind a nearby pillar, the head servant shifted, eyes narrowed, ears straining. He approached them with a fabricated excuse, announcing supper. The siblings followed obediently, blending into the evening routine, masking the storm beneath their skins.

Later, when the house was silent and the stars hung high, Ola crept back inside. Her hands moved with practiced speed as she packed dried cassava and smoked meat. Every rustle of cloth and creak of the floor heightened the urgency.

She locked the door, tucked the key beneath a flowerpot, and met her brother under the stars.

They slipped into the night like ghosts.

The parish dogs did not stir. Father Angelo's absence had silenced them. Ola silently thanked the universe. Yet her heart remained heavy, drenched in thoughts of her mother and the priest's sacrifice. She kept her eyes forward, even as her vision blurred with tears. They walked deeper into the wilderness.

As Ola and Nunu drifted towards the Ota region, Keko, the silent killer, moved with the precision of a striking serpent. His bare feet glided over roots and rocks as though the forest itself had opened a path for him. Behind him, the Nyungu warriors followed in tight formation, face painted with ash, blades strapped across their backs, eyes burning with one mission: to bring the Chief's daughter home, dead or alive. The forest swallowed their presence. No voice rose. No branch snapped too loudly. Even the wind seemed to bow in fear.

They arrived at the parish before Father Angelo's robes had brushed the outer footpath. The compound was still. The air was heavy with the scent of wet grass, burnt cassava, and faint incense. A lone lantern flickered in the chapel window, casting long shadows on cracked mud walls. Then came the shuffle of a broom dropped mid-sweep. The parish helper, an old man with trembling hands and sunken eyes, stood frozen at the door.

"They ran," he croaked. "The boy, her brother, warned her. Nunu. Said danger was coming. They slipped away just before nightfall."

Silence.

Keko didn't flinch. He didn't blink. A storm passed behind his eyes, dark, slow, and inevitable. Then came the eruption. A shout tore from one warrior's throat, primal and sharp. Another kicked over a cooking pot, sending scalding water hissing into the dirt. Keko, calm and terrifying, strode toward the chapel. His arm snapped forward. His spear tore through the chapel door like paper.

He stepped inside, eyes scanning the wooden altar, the humble benches, the crucifix on the wall. His finger brushed the carved cross before he shoved it to the floor.

The destruction came swiftly and savagely.

Boots thundered through the compound. Hymnals flew like startled birds, pages torn and flung into the air. The communion cup shattered beneath a heel, its pieces flashing like silver teeth. One warrior hurled a bench onto the altar, splintering the wood. A lantern tipped. Oil spilled. Flames bloomed. Within moments, the thatched roofs of grass caught fire. Smoke surged skyward, thick, acrid, choking the air with the smell of burning palms and prayer. Bells melted. Bees fled from nearby hives in frantic clouds. Dogs howled at the village edge.

The girl was still missing.

They combed the compound. Scoured the edge of the maize fields. Ripped the banana grove. Slashed through underbrush where footpaths might hide. No scent. Nothing but broken stems and mocking silence.

Breathless, sweating, seething, the warriors gathered at the edge of the tree line, smoke curling behind them like an omen. Keko's chest rose and fell with slow, controlled fury. He turned his gaze southward, toward home. Toward the wrath of Chief

Odu, whose commands were never questioned and whose punishments were legendary.

Without a word, the indomitable Keko started the long walk back to Nyungu, as Ola and Nunu drifted farther away.

Nunu led his sister into the oppressive quiet. The air grew denser, not just with heat but with an ominous heaviness. Shadows moved strangely. The scent of ash gave way to something fouler: wet fur, raw earth, blood long dried. Every crunch beneath their feet sounded too loud. Every breath cut was too sharp. A branch snapped, not theirs. The march slowed. Muscles tightened. The deeper they went, the more the forest pulsed with a presence not entirely human. Then the dark came alive, chirping, howling, and whispering. Then, a deeper sound: guttural breathing. Heavy. Close.

They froze.

Eyes glowing in the thicket.

Hooves.

"Stop," she whispered. "Let them pass."

Nunu gritted his teeth. "We can't stop now."

"We stop," she said firmly, pointing to a tree.

They climbed quickly and nestled in the branches.

Below, shadows moved, giant, hulking shapes with twisted horns. Buffalo. A herd.

A brittle branch cracked and broke as Nunu leaned in for a better view. He scrambled, barely catching another branch, but the damage was done. One massive bull turned its snout, sniffed, and charged.

It slammed into the tree, shaking it with each blow. Bark flew. Leaves rained. Nunu clung desperately as fear surged and his body betrayed him. A warm stream spilled downward. The bull snorted in rage as Nunu's urine fell on its back. It pawed the earth violently, then rammed the tree again.

Suddenly, snap!

Nunu fell, landing squarely on the beast's back.

The buffalo reared.

Ola screamed.

"Hold on!" she cried as she scrambled down from the tree.

But Nunu was already gripping the beast's horns, then its ears. The buffalo bellowed, bolting forward, galloping blindly. Nunu rode like a storm chaser, half in control, half in terror.

"Olaaaaaaaa!" he shouted. "Get out of the way!"

She stood frozen, then dove flat. The buffalo soared over her like a freight train. A thunderous blur surged past, dark and massive hooves slicing the air just inches above her head. The wind from its charge slapped her cheeks raw.

The clouds parted like torn cloth. The moon spilled out, full and silver, lighting the clearing in sudden blaze. Shadows fled. Every leaf, every stone, every drop of sweat gleamed as if it were midday.

Then shrill voices pierced the stillness, shouts, laughter, twigs snapping. Figures burst from the undergrowth: bare-chested boys with wild grins, arms flailing, waving sticks, flashing teeth in the moonlight. Ola blinked, her heart still pounding. What on earth were they doing here, now of all times?

But the night tugged her forward. No space for questions. Not while her breath came ragged and danger still crouched in the dark.

"Grab the tail!" one boy shouted in the Ota dialect, a language close to Nyungu.

Nunu reached for the tail but missed. Instead, he caught a low-hanging branch and swung off, hitting the ground with a thud. The buffalo did not look back.

The boys swarmed him, clapping and cheering.

"*Ogidigidi!*"

The beast rider! they chanted.

Ola arrived, panting. She found her brother weakly grinning, surrounded by admirers. But she recognized that smile. Beneath it, he was still shaken from the beast ride.

She knelt beside him and placed a hand on his shoulder.

"You're mad," she said gently.

"And you're slow," he teased.

They laughed, softly, hollowly.

The laughter faded as quickly as it had begun. One of the boys stepped forward, slim and wiry, with the sharpness of someone who had survived the wild. They would later learn his name was Kado. He crouched beside Nunu, his eyes scanning the fresh bruises and the bloody smear on his lip.

"Who sent you into these parts?" Kado asked, his voice low and cautious.

Nunu hesitated.

Ola met the boy's gaze, fierce and unflinching. "We sent ourselves."

Kado narrowed his eyes. "Strangers don't send themselves into Ota's land at night. Not unless they're running from something."

Ola's silence was her answer.

A second boy stepped up, shorter, broader, with a jagged scar slashing across his cheek. "Warrior child," he said, nodding at Nunu. "That was a mad ride. Even our bravest would think twice."

"It wasn't bravery," Nunu replied, breathless. "It was the only choice."

That silenced them.

Kado stood and signaled to the others. "Bring water. And the herbs."

Soon, Ola and Nunu were seated by a dying fire, drinking a bitter-leaf brew from calabash bowls. The other Ota boys circled like wolves, protecting the new cubs. Above them, stars blinked through the swaying tree branches. Smoke curled lazily into the night air.

CHAPTER SIX

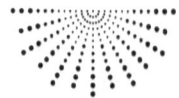

Ola shifted the bundle of firewood on her head and fell back a little from the group. Her brother and the Ota boys walked ahead, laughing as the breeze carried their voices. Now full of swagger from his buffalo tale, Nunu gestured wildly while the others hooted and slapped each other's backs. As they walked, Ola's eyes wandered, not toward the boys, but toward the land.

The path wove through a plateau dotted with acacia trees. Bright blossoms, bougainvillea among them, spilled their scent into the warm air. The occasional trill of birdsong, sweet and sudden, lifted her spirits. A bushbuck darted between the shrubs and paused to graze. She noticed a tree stump with fresh bark from a recent cut. Nearby, the charred ground whispered of a fire not long ago. Still, the land pulsated with life, aching with beauty. Ola breathed it in and let her mind drift toward home.

Was Mama safe? What about the Man of God? Her

thoughts tangled like vines. Nyungu felt far away, but her worries pressed close.

"Look, look, look! Smoke! That's home!" one of the boys cried.

The word home snapped her back. She blinked, and beyond the trees, smoke curled over a cluster of thatched roofs. A village. Her heart rate spiked. It was time to prepare a story, truth, dressed with just enough spice to pass as legend. The Otanians would not shelter strangers without reason. Luckily, she had both reason and wit.

Kado halted at the edge of the village. He turned to Ola and Nunu.

"Wait here," he said. "We'll ask for permission." The boys strode off, firewood balanced on their backs like antlers.

Ola stood still, her heart ticking loudly. In Ota, strangers were not guests. They were considered threats until proven otherwise.

After a long wait, the bushes parted. A tall man emerged beside Kado, his posture calm, eyes sharp. His face was kind but unreadable.

"I am Opio," he said. "Chief of security for Ota." He studied them with the quiet caution of someone trained to expect danger, even in young faces. "Follow me."

They stepped into the compound behind him. People poured out of the huts, dozens of them. Women in bright dresses that swirled around their ankles tilted their heads and smiled kindly, though warily. Men, taller than the Nyungu men Ola had known, leaned on spears and watched with narrowed eyes.

The village design impressed her; huts encircling a central

dwelling like petals guarding the heart of a flower. That, she guessed, was the chief's. Later, she would learn that women built these homes, fed them, stocked the markets, and then handed over the earnings to husbands who planned, hunted, and protected. It was a balance of burden, uneven but ancient.

She noticed the women's skin, shades of roasted cocoa, glowing in the sun. Their dresses caught the light like a field of flowers. The men, especially the older ones, wore only shirts, bare from the waist down. She did not stare, though curiosity tugged at her. A younger boy would later whisper that the elders believed trousers stifled growth. She left it at that.

Inside Opio's hut, Kado disappeared. When he returned, Ola realized he was Opio's son.

The chief of security retrieved his spear and beckoned them forward. They followed silently, heads lowered, through a crowd of stares and murmured questions.

Before entering the central hut, Opio drove his spear into the ground. With a voice like a drumbeat, he called the name of the Ota chief three times, announced himself, and waited for a signal.

"Welcome to my home and your home, Opio, son of Opeto," came a booming voice.

From the doorway emerged a double-chinned woman wrapped in dignity and bright cloth. Her smile was wide. Her voice was loud. "And who are these bonny tiddlers?"

"Seekers, Lioness of Opeto," Opio replied, bowing slightly. "They bring no harm, only hope."

"Come in, children of the earth," she laughed. "Come suckle the ample Opeta breast."

Opio leaned in closely.

"Speak only when spoken to. Answer only what is asked," he whispered in the official Kobole language.

Ola nodded. She caught every word. Kobole, the national tongue, bridged the tribes. For once, she was glad.

The room glowed. The walls, beadwork, paintings, and embroidery burst with color. Animal skins lined the floor. At the center, Chief Oca sat high on a carved throne, his feet resting on a leopard skin. His robes shimmered, stitched from the hides of lions, bears, and monkeys. Behind him, two warriors stood like statues, spears ready. At his feet, many wives sat in rows, sorted by age. Edema, the senior wife, held her place near him, a proud matron on a polished elephant hide. The others folded their hands in their laps, silent and still.

The air was thick. Ola's throat tightened. Nunu stood firm, jaw set. Across the room, his eyes locked with the chief's, unblinking.

Opio shifted nervously. Sweat bloomed across his brow. He motioned for Nunu to look away. Nunu didn't.

Then the lion spoke.

"Where do you come from, boy who dares meet a lion's gaze?"

Ola opened her mouth, then remembered: *only if asked*. She clamped it shut.

"Kwa Nyungu, my chief," Nunu replied.

"What brings you here with a girl?"

"We're running from circumcision."

Ola nearly groaned. Her tale, so carefully stitched, now unraveled at her brother's feet.

"Circumcision?" Oca's voice thundered. "Do men run from that?"

Nunu didn't flinch.

"No, my chief. They wanted to cut my sister."

Gasps spread among the women.

"You fled to protect her?" Oca asked.

"Yes, my chief."

Silence spread like shadows.

Ola bit her lip. She wanted to wring Nunu's neck, but he looked calm. Confident.

"What do you think, Mother of Many?" Oca asked.

Edema sat straighter.

"My lord, the boy is brave. Protecting future mothers is a noble act. They are too young to wander in danger. Let the Lion of Opeto show mercy."

Oca's face softened. He turned to his wives. Each one nodded in turn.

"Opio," he called.

The security chief dropped to his knees. "Yes, my chief."

"You will watch over them. Teach them our ways."

Opio bowed lower. "Yes, my chief."

Ola's breath returned. Her brother smiled slightly. They had made it.

They left the *boma,* the Ota chief's official hut, under the gaze of hundreds of eyes. Behind them, the leopard skin, the throne, and the man who could command storms remained still as stone. Ola felt the air shift. Something had changed. Odu's children now had a place among the Otanians.

They would stay, for a long time.

CHAPTER SEVEN

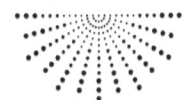

At dawn, Ota pulsed with ritual and rhythm. Ola stirred beneath a raffia mat, the cool earth grounding her more than any dream ever could. Roosters crowed from the kraal, and the smoky scent of millet porridge lingered in the air like a hymn sung by ancestors. Outside, the village came alive movement, laughter, chores, and drumming. A new day. And they were still here.

The Otanians wasted no time in making their move. Guests or not, idle hands offended the ancestors.

By mid-morning, Nunu was handed a blunt spear and tossed into a sparring ring with two boys his size and one twice his age.

"We train the weak early," said Opio, narrowing his eyes. "It helps them grow into strength, not sorrow."

Ola was led elsewhere, past the water gourd station, past the pounding stones, into an expansive courtyard where Ota women had gathered in a loose circle on a patch of flattened red earth. With baskets at their feet and clay pots beside them, women of all ages worked while their tongues danced in layered conversation.

"You will not carry firewood all day," said Edema, beckoning her to sit beside her. "You will learn what it means to build from the inside out."

She handed Ola something unfamiliar.

"What is this?"

"A bean sprout wrapped in oil and medicine. You will plant it. You will water it. When it grows, it is ground into flour. You are no longer a stranger when that flour feeds someone."

And so, it began.

Mornings blurred into routine: grinding, planting, weaving, soaking cassava in ash, scrubbing calabashes, and listening to instructions and stories. The Ota women rarely taught or explained; they showed. Correction came not through scolding, but a head tilt or a look sharp enough to cut yam. Still, they welcomed her into the rhythm of their lives, more than Ola had dared to hope for.

Nunu, too, adapted quickly. He sparred until his arms ached, fished with the river clan boys, and learned to mimic calls of the green-chested weaver. By the third week, he no longer looked like a boy helping his sister to escape the blade. He looked like someone training to wield it, on his own terms.

At night, they sat by the communal fire under the star-studded sky. Sometimes they danced. Sometimes they drummed. And sometimes they listened to old men tell stories in three languages: the Ota dialect, Kobole, and the deep guttural chants of the forest clans.

One night, Edema turned to Ola.

"You carry more than firewood on your head. You carry memory. And memory must be taught, not just felt."

That was the night Ola began learning the songs.

Not lullabies or hymns, but *truth songs,* long, winding verses that carried the history of the Ota. Each woman sang them differently. Each version was right. None was complete.

"You add your voice," Edema said, "so the story lives."

And Ola sang.

Haltingly at first. Then, with more confidence. Once tight with fear, her voice softened and widened like a river finally breaking through its banks.

Yet despite the warmth, not everything was easy. Some villagers still stared for too long and muttered too softly.

"Strangers bring curses," an old man whispered near the goat pen. "Strangers plant lies."

Once, someone left a doll at their doorstep, made of straw and charcoal, its neck was bent, its eyes were painted red.

"A curse," whispered the girls who saw it. Ola tossed it into the fire. "Let them know I do not fear straw."

But she did fear something.

The silence.

No word from Nyungu. No sign of Mama. No whispers from the Man of God.

Only the knowing glances passed between Opio and Edema when they thought the children were not watching. Only the occasional hawk feather tucked behind someone's hut, black, stiff, and ominous.

Then came the festival.

The Festival of Dry Leaves came once a year, when the wind blew from the south, and the trees shed their brittle skins. A celebration of what dies to give way to life. A time to burn old regrets, shed names, and take on new ones.

That night, around the village bonfire, every family tossed dry leaves into the flames, each representing a name, secret, or sorrow.

When Edema passed Ola a leaf, she paused.

"What will you burn?" the woman asked.

Ola stared into the flame.

"Fear," she whispered. Then louder: "Fear, and the name they used to control me."

She dropped the leaf into the fire.

The flames crackled, hissed, and flared.

Edema placed a warm palm on her back. "Then let the fire remember it. Not you."

From that night on, no one called her a stranger again.

They called her *Ola of the Ember Song*, the girl who came from smoke, walked through fire, and stayed to sing.

Thus, the children of Nyungu stayed, through the season of dry leaves, through the season of thunderclouds, and into the season of green shoots.

Ola planted her second sprout when the rains came, and it flourished. Nunu led a hunting party into the lower hills and returned with a wild hare slung proudly across his shoulders. They were no longer watched with suspicion. They were greeted with claps on the back, cups of fermented sorghum, and space by the fire.

Their limbs grew stronger. Their speech softened and bent gently into the Ota dialect. Their shadows no longer moved like guests. They danced with the moon during harvest. They helped rebuild the elder's hut after the windstorm. Ola even earned the rare honor of tracing dye patterns on the matron's new wrapper cloth, an act reserved for girls with steady hands and faithful hearts.

Time unfurled like a woven cloth.

One season folded into the next.

Then came the drums, low and steady at first, echoing from the hills.

The long-awaited harvest season had arrived.

All of Ota stirred.

Young men carved new spears and combed their hair with ceremonial oil. Girls embroidered veils and bathed in river herbs until their skin gleamed like oiled timber. The elders prepared the grounds, trimmed the fields, and stacked firewood high for the feasts.

It was a season when bloodlines merged, ancestors were praised, and every child who had once run from danger was asked:

Now that you have been planted, what will you become?

As the village spun with laughter, music, and the rustle of new cloth, Ola stood beneath the same acacia tree she had passed on that first day. Its blossoms had returned, brighter than before. She reached up, ran her fingers along the smooth bark, and smiled at the tree.

She and Nunu had arrived as fugitives.

They had remained through three full seasons.

Now, the village danced, and they danced with it.

But as the seasons changed, so too did the village's gaze.

Ola was no longer the frightened girl hiding in her brother's shadow. She had blossomed like the river lilies that unfurled after the rains, slowly, then all at once. Her beauty did not arrive with the clang of an announcement, but with the quiet insistence of dawn. Her skin was burnished mahogany, glistening with shea oil each morning. Her almond-shaped eyes held stories beneath their still surface, and when she smiled, it was like sunlight slipping through banana leaves after a storm.

Where once there had been indifference or suspicion, now there was awe. The boys of Ota tripped over their feet as she passed. They straightened their shoulders, deepened their voices, and offered carved bracelets dyed with marula bark. Some stumbled through greetings; others performed small heroics, hoisting firewood with one hand, or climbing mango trees faster than sense allowed.

Even older men noticed. Hunters returning from the hills spoke her name with the hush usually reserved for mountain spirits. Blacksmiths paused mid-hammer as her skirts swayed by like woven poetry. A scent clung to her; sometimes baobab blossoms, sometimes crushed lemongrass, always something the wind could not forget.

At the evening fires, the stories began to shift. They now spoke of a mysterious maiden whose gaze could tame a leopard or soothe a feverish child. Even the village drummers adjusted their rhythm when she joined the circle, softer, more deliberate, as though afraid her steps might vanish if startled.

Yet Ola herself moved as though untouched by the storm she stirred. She laughed freely. Hauled cassava with the other girls. Knelt beside the elders, soaking dyed cloth in silence. She didn't dance to be seen, but because the music demanded it.

And beneath the full moon, as her silhouette shifted between flame and shadow, some swore they saw the spirit of Nyungu rise in her form.

The Ota boys called her *the girl with thunder in her bones*.

But Nunu, watching from the edge of the firelight, simply called her *sister*.

And still, as the harvest ripened, the wedding drums beat louder.

CHAPTER EIGHT

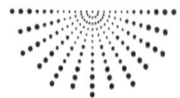

The sun, a molten orb, spilled its honeyed light across Ota village, setting the thatched rooftops aglow and gilding the dust that danced lazily in the air. Fields that once shimmered with the pale green of promise now swayed with heavy heads of millet and maize, their golden stalks rustling like whispers of fulfillment. The air was thick with the ripeness of harvest, celebration, and something ancient stirring beneath the surface.

The village pulsated with anticipation. Children raced barefoot across sunbaked earth, their feet kicking up clouds of ochre dust, their peals of laughter echoing between mud-walled huts like the call of birds at dawn. Women, their backs glistening with sweat, pounded yams in rhythm, wooden pestles thudding into mortar bowls in a cadence older than memory. The scent of roasting meat and freshly tapped palm wine wove through the village like a spell, making mouths water and stomachs churn with longing.

At the heart of it all stood the ancestral arena, once a sacred ground of invocation, now alive with color and movement. Palm fronds framed the space like banners, and the air quivered with drumbeats that thudded like a heartbeat. Young men, their torsos slick with palm oil and dust, grappled in fierce wrestling bouts. Their sinewy bodies glistened under the sun, muscles flexing like coiled ropes, faces locked in the intense focus of warriors proving themselves. Cheers erupted with every throw, twist, and fall. This was no mere contest of brawn; it was a proving ground for manhood, a test of who was worthy to lead a home, protect a family, and uphold the ancestor's legacy.

At dawn, a different ritual unfolded. A serpentine procession of maidens wound its way to the river, their white wrappers clinging to dew-kissed skin. The river, cool and silvered in the early light, welcomed them with gentle ripples. They bathed in silence, the soft splashes mingling with birdsong and the rustle of reeds. Afterwards, they emerged glowing, limbs slick with coconut oil, the sweet, nutty fragrance mingling with the earthy scent of damp soil and wildflowers. Under the vigilant gaze of elder women, they rehearsed the wedding dance hips swaying, wrists flicking, bare feet tapping in fluid rhythm. Every movement was a language; every gesture, an offering to tradition and the gods.

Among them was Ola, the one whispered about in every courtyard and marketplace. Her beauty lay not just in her almond-shaped eyes or the graceful line of her neck, but in the way she moved like a flame, unpredictable and mesmerizing. Her skin shimmered like polished mahogany in the sun. When she danced, time seemed to pause. Her laughter, rare and soft as wind chimes, stirred something primal in every man who heard it. No suitor from her settlement dared to dream of her; custom forbade it. She belonged to no man, yet belonged to them all, the embodiment of the Ota spirit.

Her heart was pledged to Mukeri, a warrior from a distant settlement. This son of thunder and smoke had emerged from the eastern plains like a storm. Towering and broad-shouldered, his presence was a challenge to silence. His voice, deep and rolling, seemed to tremble the ground. Stories followed him like loyal dogs: how he broke a spear across his knee in battle, how a charging bull once turned away beneath his gaze. When he laughed, birds scattered from the trees. When he walked, the earth seemed to remember his footsteps.

The village worked as one in preparation for the event. Married men returned with game slung over their shoulders: antelope, guinea fowl, and wild boars. Boys, their faces dusted with ash, scurried about with arms full of firewood. Little girls swept the arena, their laughter like bells, their brooms scraping the earth in rhythm. Elders stirred cauldrons of thick sorghum beer, its tangy aroma rising like an incantation. Smoke curled from cooking fires. Songs were sung. Faces were painted. Hope was tangible.

Then came the ceremony, the crown jewel of the celebration. The drums spoke first, thunderous and commanding. Grooms, robed in rich indigo, led their brides into the arena, the sun catching the gleam of their beaded necklaces and bronze bracelets. Ola walked beside Mukeri, her face veiled in sheer gold, her ankles chiming with each step. The crowd erupted. Ululations pierced the air. Onlookers clapped in rhythm. The arena exploded with color, music, and the sacred joy of union.

Amidst the revelry, an unexpected sound pierced through the night.

Gunshots.

The first crack split the sky like lightning, a violent tear in the heavens. For a heartbeat, everything froze. Drummers halted mid-beat. Dancers stopped mid-twirl. Elders turned slowly, heads cocked in disbelief.

Then came the second shot, and the world fractured. Panic tore through the crowd like a storm let loose. Women screamed, clutching their children. Calabashes shattered under frantic feet. Wedding garments, once pristine and proud, were trampled into dust, stained with sweat, tears, and blood.

Drums toppled. Spears clanged. Ululations gave way to wails. Smoke from overturned cooking pots curled upward, mixing with the sharper tang of gunpowder and the acrid sting of burning palm fronds. Goats broke loose and bolted blindly. Chicken flapped in terror. Feathers rained down like cursed snow. Elders stumbled, their ceremonial staffs abandoned in the stampede. Somewhere, a child wailed for its mother, sharp and piercing, like a flute note in a broken song.

The rebels moved with terrifying precision. Faces masked. Machetes flashing. Boots grinding sacred ground into ruin. They kicked over ancestral stools. Tore down canopies. Dragged brides by their veils. Fires sprang up, small at first, then fed by dry reeds and chaos. The arena, the sacred cradle of music and memory, became a battlefield. Cries of resistance rose. Men fought with bare fists and broken sticks. But they were outmatched. One rebel swung his rifle like a club, smashing a young groom to the ground. Another hurled a calabash of sorghum beer into the fire, triggering a blinding flash.

The spirit of the ancestors, once believed to hover above the arena, seemed to have fled alongside the villagers.

Dust. Smoke. Screams.

Ola stumbled backward through the chaos, her ears ringing not just with gunfire, but with the heartbeat of something sacred breaking. The rebels had not just interrupted a ceremony, they had desecrated memory itself.

Then came the shadows. They moved along the edges of the crowd, slow, deliberate, inhuman. And then they emerged. The NFP rebels. Their faces were streaked with soot, cloths wrapped tightly around their heads. Eyes glinted like obsidian shards. Rifles rose like skeletal limbs, their cold metal catching the firelight with murderous gleam.

A beat. Breathless. Still. Then, chaos returned with a vengeance. Screams split the air, shrill, guttural, mingling with the sharp staccato of the gunfire. Smoke thickened, curling into mouths and eyes, turning every breath into a choking struggle. People ran blindly, stumbling over calabashes, slipping on spilled palm oil, crashing into each other as the earth itself seemed to shake beneath them. Bare feet pounded the hard red soil, kicking up dust that clung to sweaty skin and burned the throat.

Mothers screamed names into the rising smoke, their voices cracking with fear as they reached out for small hands already lost in the chaos. The scent of burning grass mixed with the sharp tang of gunpowder and the heavy stench of fear. Warriors turned, searching for spears left leaning against trees or beside cooking fires, always too far away. The air pulsed with noise: shouts, sobs, clattering pots, and the sick thud of bodies hitting the ground.

The rebels came forward, silent and sure, their boots thudding with a slow, confident rhythm. This was not just an attack; it was a swallowing. A consuming. The village that once throbbed with drums, laughter, and roasting yam now reeked of smoke, sweat, fear, and the coppery promise of blood.

Ola's world spun and shattered. Rough hands clamped down on her arms, smelling of dust, iron, sweat, and iron, dragging her off-balance before she could even scream. Shadows swallowed the flickering torchlight as ropes snapped tight around her wrists, thick and scratchy, biting into her skin like curses. She fought, twisting, but the hands held firm, dragging her across sacred ground that had lost its holiness.

Her bare feet scraped over the wreckage of what had been a celebration, now a graveyard of joy. Shattered gourds crunched beneath her heels, their sweetness turning sour in the smoke. Flower crowns, once fragrant with hibiscus and jasmine, lay crushed and dirtied. Banana leaves clung to her ankles like cruel reminders. The scent of roasted yam and palm wine was gone, replaced by smoke, urine and blood. Her lungs burned. Each breath scraped her throat.

Behind her, Nunu's voice tore through the night, raw and furious. "Let her go!" it screamed. Then came a brutal thud flesh against wood? Skull against stone? Ola did not know. But the sound split the night. And then, silence. Heavy, suffocating silence. Even the drums had stopped.

In their place, the crackle of fire, sharp, greedy, unstoppable. Flames climbed the thatched roofs, shadows jerking across the walls like restless spirits. Somewhere, a flute cried. It was a high, lonely wail swallowed by the smoke, as if the air itself mourned. The torches flared, casting a harsh golden light that revealed too much: the madness in rebel eyes, terror frozen on villagers' faces, and blood smeared across the earth like desperate handprints.

The air had changed. It was pressed heavy, and foul, thick with smoke, sweat, scorched wood, and the bitter tang of fresh blood. It coated her mouth, each breath a battle.

The elders huddled, clutching their charms, their whispers frantic, prayers dragged from memory. Ash streaked their robes. Fear painted their faces. Children whimpered under benches, their small bodies trembling, their cries muffled by shaking hands.

Through it all, the rebels moved like a dark tide, uncaring and unstoppable. They stormed the sacred grounds, ignoring ancestral carvings and altars draped in ceremonial cloth. Drums were kicked apart, ritual pots shattered, ancestor stones toppled like nothing. Blades flashed, spears stabbed at shadows. Symbols of power meant nothing. What had been holy was now a battlefield.

Smoke curled heavy as torches burned and shadows danced across broken ground. Ola's wrists burned against the coarse rope, each jolt from her captor sending her stumbling through trampled flower garlands and overturned calabashes. Nunu's voice, hoarse and defiant, rose once more before being silenced by a blow. She did not dare to look back. Around her, mothers screamed for their children, warriors struggled to regroup, and elders clung to relics that could no longer protect them.

Ahead loomed the forest: dark, dense, watching. Its breath was thick with damp earth and wildflowers, heavy and strange. Towering trees crowded together, their bark rough as scars, their leaves whispering like voices from another time. Each step sank slightly in soft moss and treacherous mud. The coolness of air did not soothe, it clung, heavy as wet cloth, smelling of decay and unseen life. Behind them, the village smoldered. Ash and blood trailed faintly in the breeze. Above, the stars blinked cold and far, offering no guidance. No mercy. Silence reigned where drums once thundered and feet once pounded the red earth in rhythm. The dance was over. What remained was breath held tight, eyes wide with fear, and the forest's silent promise: pain, reckoning, and no way back.

CHAPTER NINE

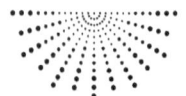

The moon faded behind the trees, but still, they trudged on, bare feet against thorns, limbs trembling, and eyes heavy with dust and despair. Not a whisper broke the silence of their march. When dawn finally crept over the horizon, the rebels halted at the edge of a clearing strewn with burnt-out huts and fading embers. In this semi-char, Mokote, the rebel leader, stood like a scar carved into the morning light. He was lean, coiled, and battle-worn. His skin was a dark map of old wounds and newer rage, stretched tight over sinew and bone. A jagged burn traced his jawline, curving into his beard like an untold story. His eyes, black and unblinking, held the cold patience of a lion watching its prey.

He wore no insignia, only a threadbare scarf wrapped around his wrist, the blood-red mark of those with nothing to lose. When he shifted slightly, even the forest seemed to flinch. Even the wind avoided him as he walked.

The moment he spotted the Olas, Mokote raised his fist.

They halted mid-step. He pressed a crooked finger to his lips, eyes sweeping the terrain like a hungry predator. With a flick of his wrist, three shadows melted into the ruins, scouting the stillness. Moments later, a slight nod from one of the scouts beckoned the group to move. The rebels slipped into the hollow camp like ghosts, dragging their captives behind them. The prisoners collapsed to the ground the moment they entered. The earth welcomed their weight as they fell. They didn't speak. Couldn't. Their mouths were too dry, their bodies too brittle. Hunger gnawed at their bellies, but the silence of the day was law. It was the rebels' cloak against government patrols. For the abductees, this forced stillness was a kind of mercy.

When daylight fully stretched across the camp, Ola saw what she had not dared to imagine. The place teemed with fellow captives, dozens, maybe hundreds, of every age and status. Tiny children still clung to their mothers' shriveled breasts. The elderly stood barely upright, their eyes empty. The chiefs and servants huddled together like cattle. The rebels had cast a wide net under the cover of night, taking whomever they could catch. Suffering, Ola realized, respected no title.

Her eyes wandered and then stopped.

Near the charred remains of a grass-thatched hut sat a figure too familiar to mistake. Mukeri. Her fiancé. The man whose wrestling triumph had once shaken the village. The giant of that day had shriveled into something smaller, something less. The rope dug into his wrists. His proud head hung in shame. Though rage still pulsed beneath his skin, shame wrapped around him tighter than any knot.

A shiver crept up Ola's spine. Someone was behind her.

She turned, and there he was standing.

Mokote.

His gaze bored into her. His bloodshot eyes glowed like embers. He leaned in, and the world shrank to the stench of his breath, sour with rot, tobacco, and weeks without water. His yellowed, jagged teeth peeked through a half-smile twisted with mockery. As he stuffed a wad of tobacco into his mouth with filthy fingers and began to chew, the sound was obscene, like wet gravel grinding. Ola almost gagged. But fear held her tongue hostage.

He stared, unblinking, then spat a brown stream that hissed onto the ground between them. His leer deepened into a wink. Then, just as suddenly, he turned and stalked off toward Mukeri, his ragged trousers dragging behind him like a second skin.

Ola caught her breath. Around her, the other captives exhaled; the collective relief was almost audible. She glanced at Nunu. Her brother's eyes were ablaze, his muscles taut. He looked one heartbeat away from snapping his rope and lunging forward. But something or someone had kept him tethered. She swallowed hard. That invisible leash had just saved his life.

Mokote strutted toward Mukeri, his stick tapping the ground with the slow menace of authority. Like a herdsman, he poked at the other captives, and when one flinched or resisted, he beat them without mercy. Then he stopped in front of Mukeri.

"Up," he barked.

Mukeri didn't move.

"Stand!" Mokote roared, louder now, demanding submission.

Slowly, Mukeri lifted his chin and rose, deliberately, like a prince still clinging to his crown. His towering frame dwarfed Mokote's. His silence was its own defiance. Mokote's face twisted with fury.

"You big-for-nothing ox!" Mokote spat. "Stubborn lump of meat!"

Mukeri snorted.

That was enough.

In a flash, the rebels descended on him. Sticks cracked against flesh. Dust and sweat burst into the air. Groans gave way to screams, screams to whimpers, and whimpers to silence.

Still, they did not stop.

All around, cries erupted, children sobbed, mothers wailed, and elders muttered prayers. Mokote turned, his face twitching with rage, and pointed at the crowd.

"Beat them all!"

And the storm spread.

Pain danced across the camp. The rebels laughed, their joy cruel and wild. Bamboo rods whistled through the air, landing with sickening thuds on backs, legs, shoulders. When Mukeri's battered body finally stopped twitching, he lay face-down in the dirt, soaked in blood. Breathless. Mokote sauntered over and drove his boots into the ribs. The body did not flinch.

Satisfied, the rebel chief raised his arm. The beatings ceased. He scanned the camp. Bloodied faces. Crushed spirits. But silence had returned.

"Listen well!" he bellowed. "From now on, I own your lives. Disobey me, and you'll end like this useless dog."

He jabbed his foot at Mukeri's corpse.

"These ropes on your wrists? They now go to your necks.

You'll be grouped. Fifty per rope. That is your new family. And from tonight, we work."

Kolobah, his second-in-command, barked commands. The rebels moved quickly, untying captives and sorting them like livestock. Strong men, women, and even teenagers were yoked together by the neck, five by five. Ola and Nunu were among them.

The elderly, the weak, and mothers with babies were placed in the fifth group.

Mokote named the units after rebel battalions: Simba, Jogo, Pepe, and Sula. Then, turning to the fifth group, he said coldly, "Forgiven. That's your name."

The "Forgiven" erupted in joy, relief washing over their faces. But Ola's heart sank. Too easy. Too kind.

The rebels began loading supplies onto the strongest backs, their movements brisk and unrelenting. One group after another was dispatched into the shadowy depths of the Kiki forest, with the so-called Forgiven leading the way.

Then came the gunshots.

Rapid. Ruthless.

Screams tore through the trees, women pleading, children shrieking. Ola froze. Her stomach twisted.

Mokote walked ahead, a smirk spreading across his tobacco-stained grin.

"They're devils," she whispered.

Nunu turned to her. His eyes were blank. Hollow. Something had died inside him. Around them, the other captives looked the same. Souls stripped bare.

Blood darkened the dust where Mukeri had fallen, now just a fading stain for the wind to scatter. Flies buzzed in drunken spirals above his crumpled form, while the dry laughter of hyenas echoed through the brush, a mockery. No one looked back. The captives trudged forward in silence, the rhythm of their chains swallowed by the growing hush. On the horizon, the trees of the Kiki Forest loomed like waiting shadows, twisted, still, and too quiet to be real. Something sinister and ancient seemed to be watching from within.

CHAPTER TEN

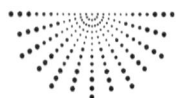

The Kiki Forest loomed ahead, a dense, shadowy expanse where sunlight dared not intrude. Locals whispered of its eerie stillness, calling it "the devil's tummy", a place where spirits dwelled and from which no one ever returned. Some revered it as sacred; others feared it as cursed.

A chill ran down Ola's spine as they approached the forest's edge. Mokote's barked orders propelled the group into the thicket, where the forest seemed to awaken with unsettling noise. Branches snapped. Unseen creatures rustled. Shadows danced at the edge of sight. Ola's imagination conjured predators lurking just beyond vision. Sweat beaded on her brow, not from exertion, but from the oppressive, watching stillness.

After two days and nights of grueling travel, the group halted near the Kholo River. A low, continuous rumble signaled its presence long before they saw it. The rebels, unfazed, prepared to cross. The captives hesitated. Mokote, with a cruel grin, ordered them into the water, threatening death to anyone who hesitates.

The river's initial shallowness was deceptive. As they moved forward, the currents strengthened, and the water deepened. Panic surged among those who could not swim, plunging the crossing into chaos. Ola and her brother Nunu drew on their childhood swimming skills to navigate the treacherous currents. Cries for help echoed as bodies vanished beneath the surface. The river, indifferent, claimed whom it pleased.

Upon reaching the far bank, the survivors collapsed, drenched and gasping. Mokote, already seated, mocked their weakness. Ola caught the hunger in his leer, and it only sharpened her resolve for vengeance. A headcount revealed significant losses on both sides. Whispers of crocodile attacks spread through the camp, evoking a mixture of horror and grim satisfaction among survivors.

Mokote's fury flared. He beat his own men, blaming them for the deaths. His unpredictability kept everyone tense, their nerves fraying. Later, he ordered the establishment of a temporary camp using forest resources. Then, in a rare and bewildering moment, he praised the captives for their effort, words of gratitude that unsettled more than they comforted.

By morning, he initiated a brutal training regimen. After forced immersion in the icy river, the captives were drilled relentlessly, including running, crawling through thorny underbrush, and performing synchronized frog jumps. Any misstep earned savage punishment. Ola's schooling proved advantageous. She understood commands that others misread, sparing herself pain and punishment.

Amid the brutality, something unexpected began to bloom: a strange, fragile camaraderie. Mokote's fiery speeches on justice and liberation began to stir questions in some, muddying the line between captor and cause. Once determined only to escape, Ola now found herself adapting. Each day sharpened her endurance, and her resilience hardened.

On the fourth night, silver moonlight threaded through the treetops. Ola sat apart from the others, her back against a mossy trunk, her gaze fixed on the stars barely visible through the canopy. Her body throbbed from exertion, but her mind churned, haunted by memories of home and the uneasy sense that something inside her was changing. Nunu approached and dropped silently beside her.

"You're becoming like them," he whispered.

Ola flinched.

"No," she said tightly. "I'm surviving."

Nunu shook his head, eyes glistening. "Survival shouldn't mean forgetting who we are."

She said nothing. But his words pierced her, lodging deep within.

Later that night, Mokote summoned her. Wordlessly, she followed him down a narrow trail that opened into a clearing lit by fireflies and a flickering torch. There, an elder rebel sat cross-legged, his eyes milky with age, flanked by two armed boys.

"She's the one," Mokote said.

The elder's gaze felt like it could peel her apart.

"You speak the enemy's language. You write. You listen. That makes you dangerous, or useful."

Ola didn't respond.

The elder gestured to a bundle, which included a leather-bound notebook, maps, and a radio.

"We need someone to decode intercepted messages. And deliver our terms to the capital if the time ever comes."

Confused and suspicious, Ola asked, "Why me?"

Mokote smirked.

"Because you're not like the rest. You're a fighter hiding in a girl's skin."

The offer, or demand, hung heavy in the humid air. Ola's pulse pounded. She could refuse and risk death or worse consequences. Alternatively, she could accept and get closer to Mokote's secrets. Perhaps close enough to destroy him entirely.

"I'll do it," she said quietly.

Mokote clapped triumphantly. The elder only nodded. Inside, Ola's resolve was steeled into something sharper than survival. If she played this right, she would not only escape but also bring down the entire operation.

By the end of the week, she had memorized the rebel codes, ciphers formed from Swahili, Arabic, and the ancient Ota tongue spoken only by elders and warriors. She learned fast, too fast. Mokote noticed. He began bringing her to strategy meetings, letting her listen to southern front transmissions, watching her face like a predator searching for the glint of betrayal. Ola gave him nothing.

At night, she listened to static-laced messages, scribbling cryptic phrases and cross-referencing notebooks. Mokote did not know she was slipping in her own codes, messages buried in the margins of reports, sometimes etched in invisible ink made from resin and lemon juice.

Only Nunu knew.

"You're playing with fire," he warned one night as they huddled by the fire pit. "If he catches even a whisper of this. . . ."

"He won't," said Ola flatly. "And if he does, then we burn him first."

CHAPTER ELEVEN

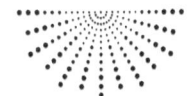

For three months, the forest had been her world; its shadows her training ground, its dangers her daily test. Each morning, Mokote watched her from a distance, arms folded across his chest. She moved like a spirit of war: silent, precise, unflinching. She did not flinch when thunder cracked overhead nor blink when a live bullet ricocheted too close. Orders? She obeyed them without question. Tasks? She completed the tasks before the next breath. No excuses. No fear. No weakness.

What began as lust burning in Mokote's eyes slowly transformed into something else: a reluctant reverence. He saw the storm behind her silence and the leadership behind her discipline. She was no longer just another girl ripped from her life, she was a commander in waiting. He began assigning her responsibilities that required more than brute strength: record-keeping, logistics, strategy. She never failed him.

But admiration breeds jealousy.

The older rebels noticed. Especially Captain Kuku and his shadow, Kiri. They saw the nods Mokote gave her in passing and the faint grin that tugged at his lips when she saluted. Resentment fermented behind their sneers. One whispered plan led to another. Soon, a lesson was plotted, one they hoped she would never forget.

That evening, Mokote summoned her and the three men. She sensed something was off as she stepped into the firelit clearing. His eyes glinted with a mix of warning and amusement.

"You four," Mokote barked. "Tonight, you raid. Food, medicine, whatever you can carry. Bring the girl back alive."

He paused.

"If she tries to run . . . shoot. Bring me an ear. Understood?"

The words slapped her. The men snapped salutes. "Yes, sir!"

Ola echoed them, voice robotic and hollow. Her body moved before her mind could catch up, a reflex honed by countless drills and discipline.

At supper, she and Nunu sat shoulder-to-shoulder. Close, but cautious. Since Mokote's rage had ended her marriage, they avoided drawing attention. But tonight was different.

"I'm going on a raid," she whispered.

Nunu's spoon froze mid-air.

"No."

She shook her head. "I have to."

"I'll talk to him."

"You won't."

He clenched his fists, and his knuckles whitened. "This feels wrong."

"It is," she said softly. "But I'll be fine."

His voice trembled as he spoke. "Don't run, Ola. Please."

"I won't," she lied, then quoted scripture: "Unless the Lord guards the house, the watchmen stay awake in vain."

Despite himself, Nunu smirked. "Don't preach to me. Just come back to me."

She squeezed his hand under the table, stood, and left. Her steps were steady, but her heart cracked with each step. It was their first time apart, the first step in what would become a nightmare.

By 9:00 p.m., they slipped into the dark. She did not look back, but she felt Nunu's eyes burning between her shoulder blades.

With every step into the darkness, her heartbeat grew louder than her boots. The air thickened. Shadows twisted into shapes that whispered threats. She did not trust the path. She did not trust the trees either. She did not trust the men who flanked her. Rifles slung casually, as if they were not already rehearsing her death.

The trek was long. The forest hummed with owls, insects, and distant howls. The men moved like ghosts through the underbrush. She matched their pace, remaining silent and alert. Her eyes adjusted to the darkness. Her ears sharpened.

By 11:00, the town appeared as a patchwork of flickering lamps, drunken songs, and late-night laughter. They waited in the shadows, crouched among the thorny bushes, watching the town wind down like a dying clock. When silence finally settled, they crept forward.

Two by two, they slipped through the night. Rifles gleamed under starlight. Their targets were careless: sacks of food, fruit baskets, and bundles of grain left outside the mud huts. In an hour, they were loaded and ready to return.

Barely inside the forest, Kuku muttered something in a dialect that Ola could not understand. She watched their faces carefully. Their faces tightened. Frowns. Sharp whispers. Eyes darted toward her.

Is this it?

Koleko, young and nervous, argued back, his voice rising, hands gesturing wildly. But Kuku silenced him with a sneer. Koleko threw up his hands and stomped ahead, sulking.

The group walked in silence. Thirty minutes later, they stopped again.

Too soon.

Kuku's voice was gruff. "Put it down. Now."

She lowered her sack slowly.

"Come here."

One heartbeat at a time, she stepped forward.

"Strip."

She froze.

"Now. Or I say you tried to run."

Her fists clenched. Her chest rose and fell, slow, controlled, burning.

She scanned their faces. Kuku, leering. Kiri, ravenous. Koleko stood aside, his face crumpled in guilt.

Two attackers. One spectator. One chance.

She slowly unbuttoned her shirt. Her bare chest gleamed in the moonlight. Kuku's breath hitched. Kiri's mouth parted, drooling at the corner.

Kuku leaned in.

This is when the storm broke.

Her clenched fist cracked his jaw like a pistol shot. Teeth flew. Blood sprayed. He screamed, producing a wet choking sound.

Before he hit the ground, her boot crushed Kiri's groin. He collapsed with a guttural cry. She wasn't done. Another kick. Then another. He folded like paper.

Koleko stood frozen, wide-eyed. She stepped toward him.

A dark patch spread down his trousers.

She stopped. "That's enough," she muttered.

Behind her, the once-mighty captains whimpered on the ground, curled up like children.

"Forgive us," they stammered through broken teeth.

She picked up her gun.

Odu's daughter, remember? You don't get to teach me lessons.

Kuku groaned on the ground, his bloody mouth trying to speak. "Forgive...."

Ola stepped forward.

Both men flinched and shielded their faces. "No more! Please!"

The clearing held its breath.

At the jungle's edge, two men stood, battered and bent, their eyes hollow with shame. Their uniforms were stained, and their dignity leaked from every wince and limping step. Behind them walked the girl, unmarked, upright, and dragging the weight of three rifles slung across her back like hunting trophies.

Ola's boots crunched softly over the leaf-littered path as she closed the distance between them. The battered soldiers dared not to meet her eyes.

"On your feet," she ordered sharply, her voice slicing

through the air like a blade. "Straighten your spines. You're still breathing, aren't you?" No one answered. She paced before them, chin high. Sunlight caught on the rifle slung across her shoulder. "From now until we reach camp, I am the commander." They flinched. "You'll carry all the supplies, including mine. And stop that sniveling." Her eyes darkened, and her voice curled with scorn. "If I'd really beaten you, you'd still be kissing dirt."

A breath hitched. A bruise deepened. A tear fell.

She smirked. "How are you feeling?"

No response.

"Good," she said, stepping aside and kicking the bags toward the men. "Take these. Divide the load. Quickly. We're late already."

They scrambled to obey and groaned under the weight. Ola watched them hoist her packs onto their sore shoulders and limp ahead. She followed them, the rifles swaying on her back in time with her stride. Two of the men limped pitifully, dragging their feet through the underbrush. Kaleko, unharmed, moved steadily and silently. He thanked the ancestors under his breath. They were lucky dawn had broken. The morning light was now beginning to spill through the canopy, casting long shadows on the jungle floor.

The trail opened into Simba's camp.

Mokote was mid-sentence when the sight stopped him cold. Around him, his comrades dropped their tools, rifles, and food. The camp froze. There stood Ola. Not behind her seniors but herding them. Kuku's face bruised. Kiri's pride shattered. Kaleko looked like he had just seen a ghost. But Ola looked as if she had been carved from stone: unbothered and victorious.

Mokote's lips parted, but the words were jammed in his throat. He blinked. His eyes fell on the rifles bouncing against her back. "Circle," he barked.

The rebels formed a wide ring around the four newcomers. On trial, Ola and the men stood at the center, exposed like animals in a pit.

"What happened?" Mokote demanded. "Why are you late? Why is the commander bleeding? Why is Ola carrying the guns?"

No one answered.

Kuku then stepped forward. "J . . . Jambo, sir," he stammered, "we're late . . . because of her, sir. She tried to escape . . . like you said she might have. We ran after her. Got her. Lost my teeth in the struggle, sir."

Mokote raised an eyebrow. "Struggle?"

Kuku nodded.

"Then why," Mokote said slowly, voice tightening, "does the girl who tried to escape come back carrying your guns? Why does she look like the one in charge?"

Nunu could not hold back. "Ask him, wise one!"

One glare from Mokote silenced him.

Kuku's mouth opened and then closed.

Mokote's eyes shifted. "Kaleko?"

The young man stood tall. His voice was clear and steady.

"After the mission, sir, Captain Kiri gave an order. Said that we should punish Ola. Said . . . she'd taken your favor from us." He paused. "I refused. But he and Commander Kuku attacked her anyway."

The silence was electrifying.

"She fought back," Kaleko said, recalling the incident. "Alone. She overpowered them. Made them beg."

A snort shattered the stillness of the arena. Then a chuckle. Suddenly, laughter burst through the camp. Mokote doubled over, slapping his knee, tears streaming down his face. Around him, the rebels roared with delight. Even the trees seemed to lean in, curious and amused by the scene.

When the laughter died down, Mokote wiped his eyes and turned to Ola.

"Your version."

Without a word, she stepped forward and reached into her waistband. From it, she drew two military peeps, badges of rank, torn clean from Kuku and Kiri's uniforms. She held them out. Mokote took the insignia, turned them over his hand, then lifted his head.

"Attention," he barked.

The four stood straight.

Mokote paced, his voice low and deliberate.

"In this jungle, justice is not a whisper. It is a roar."

He turned sharply.

"Ola has no case to answer. She defended herself. She upheld the honor of this army better than those who were sworn to lead it."

He pointed to the Kuku and Kiri.

"You are stripped of your rank. Effective immediately. You will receive one hundred lashes and two weeks of hard labor."

Gasps. Murmurs.

"You brought shame to the cause. This will be your reminder."

Then, to Kaleko, "You kept your hands clean. Therefore,

you are spared. But remember this: watching injustice without acting is betrayal. Think on that, young man."

He turned once more, this time to Ola.

"This girl. . . ." he began, then paused, correcting himself. "This woman stood against your violence, your pride, your arrogance, and she did not flinch."

He stepped forward and placed the torn insignia in her hand.

"I hereby promote Ola, daughter of Odu, to the rank of Captain. She will serve as deputy commander of Simba B Battalion."

The jungle erupted. Fists flew to the sky. Drums pounded. Shouts echoed through the trees. The air trembled with triumph. Ola stood frozen. Captain? The word did not feel real to her. Just hours ago, she had been hunted, threatened, and marked for pain. And now . . . now this.

She clenched the insignia, its sharp metal edge digging into her palm. "Think what you will, Ola," she whispered. "Mokote has spoken. And his word is final." Thus, in a single heartbeat, under a jungle sun, amid the roar of rebels, Ola, daughter of indomitable Odu, granddaughter of never-say-die Ode, became Captain. Just like that. In the blink of an eye.

CHAPTER TWELVE

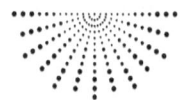

The morning air buzzed with the rhythmic cadence of drills. Captain Ola's voice rang out, sharp and commanding: "At ease, attention. At ease, attention. Quick march! Quick march! One-two, one-two. Aboooout turn!"

The recruits snapped into position, their boots thudding in unison on the hard-packed earth.

Ola stood tall, uniform crisp, eyes scanning the line of soldiers. Gone were the days when her brother called her "sir" in jest. Now, voices called her "Mum" with genuine respect, a directive from Mokote that had taken root within the camp. She offered a faint smile. The weight of leadership sat heavy, but not unwelcome, on her shoulders as she instructed recruits.

Ever the spirited one, Nunu puffed out his chest with pride as he led drills in her absence. "Remember," he'd say, grinning, "I'm the Captain's brother," a mischievous twinkle in his eye. Ola watched him, heart swelling with both amusement and affection.

Within the jungle council, Colonel Mokote, Captain Ola, and Lieutenants Patti and Bongo Lobo shaped the movement's course. As second-in-command, Ola stood at the center of strategy sessions. Her strict discipline earned her respect, but it was her keen insight that won Mokote's trust.

One morning, he led her deep into the forest, revealing a hidden cave teeming with vital supplies. The mystery of his frequent disappearances unraveled before her.

These secret meetings became routine. The council gathered regularly to inventory caches, transmit messages, and plan movements. With each session, Ola's understanding of the NFP deepened, and so did her resolve.

Kiki morphed from a makeshift camp into something closer to home. Recruits who once trembled now bore arms with confidence. Training sharpened their bodies and minds. By the river, beneath the cover of its babbling, they honed their shooting skills, their laughter mingling with the staccato of gunfire. Each carried their weapon with a new swagger; the weight was no longer a burden but a badge of honor.

But tranquility never lingered long.

A sudden radio transmission shattered the calm: Kolokolo's government had secured advanced weaponry. The council convened. Tension hung thick. Ola, her eyes narrowed in thought, proposed a daring plan. The plan was to infiltrate the Kemu police station and seize its arsenal. The tent buzzed with murmurs and nods. Mission Kemu was born, with Ola at its head.

Sleep abandoned her in the following nights. She walked the camp's edge, mapping strategies in her mind. Finally, she approached Mokote and requested a gathering of key Simba members to unveil her plans.

Disguised as a madwoman, she would enter Kemu. Nunu, posing as a vegetable vendor, would gather intelligence.

Mokote listened, then shook his head gently. "Your plan is sound, Captain. But Nunu stays. We need him here."

Lieutenant Koleko added, "You're the best suited for this mission."

Ola nodded, determination hardening her face.

Drawing from her Nyungu upbringing, she crafted weapons with meticulous care, zugu sticks honed to deadly points, their tips laced with venom from the elusive kiria snake. She braided snares from sisal, cleaned her AK-47 to a shine, and packed provisions: roasted cassava, smoked goat meat, wild nuts, each selected with precision.

Before her departure, Mokote summoned her and handed over a compass and a worn map of Kobole. "Guard these well," he said, his eyes heavy with something unspoken. "Journey mercies."

As dusk settled, she embraced Nunu, his silent tears dampening her shoulder. The camp fell into hushed reverence as she saluted Mokote, turned on her heel, and vanished into the forest.

The nocturnal journey was quiet. The moon paved silver paths through the trees.

At 3:00 a.m., she reached a familiar clearing, ghosts of past battles lingering in the stillness. She rested briefly beneath a muvule tree, her breath steadying and thoughts gathering.

She chose an unconventional route into Kemu. Along the way, she laid her traps: venom-tipped stakes beneath thick foliage, snares hidden in shadows, and a carefully disguised pitfall. Her work was seamless and each trap a testament to her skill.

By 5:00 a.m., the Kemu outskirts came into view. She concealed her weapon, donned tattered clothes, and smeared dirt across her face. A glance in a shard of glass reflected her finally transformation: The captain was gone. In her place stood a madwoman, unhinged, unreadable, and ready to gather the intelligence they so desperately needed.

CHAPTER THIRTEEN

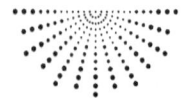

"Wake up! Wake up, sleepy heads! The town is on fire!"

The cry knifed through the velvet silence of dawn, scattering birds from trees and jolting windows ajar. Doors banged open. Bare feet slapped the dusty ground. Half-dressed men and women tumbled out of their homes, eyes wild, hearts drumming, and faces twisted in fear. But instead of smoke and flames, they found her.

At the heart of the frenzy, a young woman spun in place, shrieking with laughter that bent her double. Her hair shot out in wild, tangled strands. A rope tied around her waist dragged a clattering trail of cans, rags, and broken tins, dancing obediently behind her like a chaotic tail.

"Fire?" someone gasped.

She twirled faster. Her faded dress, smeared with dust and torn at the hem, flared with each twist. At one point, she yanked at the collar as if she meant to strip bare right in the open. Mothers shrieked. Fathers shoved children behind doorframes.

"Go inside! Don't look!"

But Ola only grinned wider, her teeth gleaming like a challenge. She threw her arms in the air and belted out an off-key tune at full volume, her hips jerking in a manic dance.

"Shut up, you cracked broom!" someone shouted.

"Do that again, and we'll beat you into the next market day!"

She sang louder.

The racket clawed its way through the entire town. Lights flickered in the distant huts. Even the goats bleated in confusion. By the time four officers in crumpled uniforms stormed onto the scene, the whole town was groggy, irritated, and thoroughly awake.

The tallest officer, lean, square-jawed, and clearly the boss, stepped forward. "You. What's your name?"

Ola blinked and tilted her head like an inquisitive owl. "What's your name?" she mimicked.

"Where are you from?" he barked.

"Where are you from?" she sang back sweetly.

The sergeant's jaw tightened. "Why do you answer questions with questions?"

"Why not?" Ola chuckled, her eyes sparkling like a trickster's.

"You're mad," Officer Polo, according to the badge on his chest, grunted, clearly done.

"Of course I am," she snapped. "So are you. You're just delaying its activation."

That cracked the dam. The frayed crowd erupted into

laughter. Even Polo's mouth twitched before he could stop it. Then, before anyone could say another word, Ola burst back into song, spinning and stomping in the dust like a woman possessed.

One by one, the onlookers melted away, muttering and chuckling. Soon, only the police officers remained. They exchanged uncertain glances. Polo stared for a little longer. Something about her did not sit right. Her madness felt . . . too organized. Too precise. But what could he say? Lunacy wore many faces. He shrugged off this discomfort.

"Back to base. Drill starts soon," he barked.

They obeyed, boots crunching as they left her behind.

He lingered. Watched. She tossed a rag into the air, caught it with her teeth, and let out a wailing banshee shriek. Still, his gut whispered: *Off. Something's off.* But duty tugged harder. With one last glance, Polo turned and walked away, whistling a hollow tune that faded into the morning mist.

When he was gone, Ola slowed her dance. Her eyes darted as she assessed the situation. Breath evened. Smile sharpened. The performance was peeled back layer by layer. Her spine straightened. Her expression turned keen and calculating. The fox had entered the henhouse. Ola scanned the town, crumbling colonial buildings, crooked verandas, rusted roofs. Not so small after all. Polo had vanished beyond the bend.

Ola, the daughter of dust and thunder, shed her madness like a cloak. With the uniformed men out of sight, her shoulders dropped slightly, and her wary eyes softened. She surveyed her surroundings with the precision of a hawk circling above a field. Kemu had shaken off its slumber and now buzzed like a restless beehive.

"Morning, mama!" echoed from one corner, followed by the clatter of sandals and the rustling of heavy market baskets. The chaos she had stirred hours earlier had already become yesterday's ghost, fading behind smirks and sideways glances from a few curious passersby.

She didn't flinch. Instead, she let her eyes roam, drinking in every flicker of life and imprinting scenes onto the reels of her photographic memory. Women shuffled past, baskets perched high, voices full of rhythm, talking of rainfall, aching husbands, and children's mischief. Conversely, men walked stiffly and unsmiling, murmuring about border clashes, troop movements, and the Kobole regime. Spy gear was unnecessary when people gave away their stories with every step.

Even in her ragged disguise, her femininity cast ripples. A handful of men slowed their pace, sneaking second glances, the corners of their mouths twitching with interest. Ola smirked. She mused that men see curves before character, even in dirt and madness.

By afternoon, the sun cast long shadows across Kemu's cracked roads. Ola had scanned nearly every corner of the town, except the police station. She saved the lion's den for last. Across from the outpost, an ancient muvule tree stretched its roots and shade like a sentry. Quietly, she slipped away from the children tailing her, lost them in the alley maze, and drifted across the road with her junk-laden rope trailing like a loyal pet.

She dropped onto her makeshift scrap throne at the tree's base, her back to the station. No one gave her a second look. Just another madwoman beneath a tree. Perfect camouflage.

From her perch, Ola slowly pivoted. The station was a portrait of lethargy. An officer lounged at the entrance, his head bowed into his chest, snoring softly. A high-caliber rifle leaned against the wall beside him, unattended. Her eyes narrowed. A sitting duck armed to the teeth is still a duck, she thought.

The door creaked. Sergeant Polo stepped out, the same bull-shouldered officer from earlier. He struck a match, lit a hand-rolled cigarette, and exhaled slowly, his gaze drifting lazily. After a few drags, he flicked the stub, stomped it with his boot, and disappeared back inside, unbothered by the guard's slumber or the silent watcher across the street.

Ola counted eight officers in total. None moved with urgency. They drifted like sleepy bulls, dragging their feet as though each step cost them a year. Even their youth sagged under the weight of apathy. Occasionally, a villager wandered in to report a stolen chicken or a broken fence. Otherwise, the station dozed in silence.

After three hours under the tree, Ola rose and brushed leaves off her skirt. The market was her next destination. Her morning had already taught her that the Kemu mamas carried more intel than any soldier. But as she approached the sprawling stalls, the clamor died down. Vendors were packing up. The sun was slipping toward the horizon.

She sighed, her lips pursed in disappointment. She promised herself that she would do it tomorrow. "Tomorrow, I return." But fate, ever the trickster, had already begun scribbling its own ending.

The sun dipped low. With the market closed, she turned to a new hunting ground: the bar. As dusk crept across Kemu, she circled back to her stash, supplies wrapped in a filthy shawl tucked under a forgotten shed. The night cloaked her like a familiar friend. In the dark, tongues loosen. She knew alcohol was the oldest spyglass in the world. "Wine fills the mouth but empties the soul," her father used to say. But Ola disagreed. What spills from a drunk's lips is the truth that sober hearts dare not speak.

She slipped into another character's shoes. In quick, precise motions, she scrubbed away the dust and sweat with a tin of water. Over her damp skin, she slipped on a crisp purple dress, simple, neat, unremarkable. Black shoes with worn soles followed. A faint scent of cheap perfume dotted behind her ears. Then came the wig. Her fingers found the hidden pouch stitched inside, where she tucked the compass and the creased, fading map. With trembling hands, she pressed her unruly hair beneath the cap, smoothing it as best she could.

Outside, shadows pooled in corners. Perfect.

She reached into her bag and pulled out roasted wild nuts, their scent earthy and nutty. She poured them into a battered basket she had swiped from a veranda. Beneath the nuts lay her pistol, its cool barrel hidden under the shell casings. A large spoon rested atop the pile, steadying the cloth cover. She balanced the basket on her wigged head, tightening the strap beneath her chin. The leather of the hidden map and compass pressed against her scalp.

She started walking.

The Nightlife Bar stood at the edge of Kemu's north end, near the police station. It pulsed with laughter, clinking glasses, and the acrid smoke of half-lit cigars. That was where masks cracked. Where secrets spilled. She was not just walking toward a drink. She was walking straight into the underbelly of Kemu's truth. Familiar faces from her earlier antics waved her down to buy nuts. Compliments laced with flirtation trailed behind. Each smile deepened the dimples in her cheeks, the cleft in her chin catching the faint light like a valley.

Odu's words echoed in her mind: "He who asks a question is a fool for a minute, but he who does not remains a fool forever." So, it pushed her curiosity, sharp as a blade, urging her to slip questions between sales, light and casual, careful not to rouse suspicion.

Her steps slowed as she approached the police station. A lanky officer stood in the doorway, arms crossed, eyes half-lidded with boredom. Her heart urged her to draw close, to glance at the station, but a flicker of caution froze her in place. The old saying flickered in her mind: "Curiosity killed the cat . . . but satisfaction brought it back." Then came the sharper warning: "The goat who saluted the hyena didn't live to tell the tale." She swallowed the urge and slipped past the harsh electric lights, and melted into the shadows.

Only the station and the bar glowed under the hum of generators. The rest of the village lay wrapped in darkness. The dim light blurred the outlines of her watchful eyes and masked her approach. Cloaked in shadows, she lingered near the station, unseen even as the officers moved in the glare of the lamps. Finally, she moved in the direction of the bar.

A jagged neon sign blinked overhead like a wounded eye: NIGHT LIFE. Pink and blue flickers bled into the thick night air. Neon tubes wound around the rusted bar frame, casting jumpy shadows across the cracked pavement. The music slammed against the walls like fists, the bassline pulsing so hard that the ground beneath Ola's feet trembled. She paused across the street, swallowed by the darkness, arms around the basket.

Her eyes did not move from the entrance. *Wait,* she told herself. *Just wait.*

She watched bodies funnel in and out of the club, dancing, shouting, and staggering. Massive speakers flanked the entrance, thundering so loudly that speech became noise. You had to scream to be heard, and even then, your voice dissolved into the beat. Her fingers tightened around the basket. Beneath the roasted nuts, hidden beneath the cloth lining, was her gun. She exhaled slowly to steady the tremble in her gut. She then stepped into the neon.

The light slapped her sharply and mercilessly as she stepped outside. Her eyes shrank against the assault, pain stinging behind her eyelids. She blinked rapidly, but the night offered no reprieve. The bouncer guarding the entrance was thick-chested, all brawn and sweat. His eyes flicked to her and lingered. He licked his lips.

"Angel eyes like those?" he said, leaning close enough for her to smell the alcohol soaked into his breath. "Can't be a threat." She didn't respond. He stepped aside and smirked. "Be sure to sell me some nuts on your way out."

She gave him a soft, neutral smile, sweet enough to pacify but sharp enough to unsettle. Then she slipped past him and entered the bar. Inside, chaos reigned.

Flashing lights sliced through the crowd. The dance floor writhed with bodies, skin-to-skin, drinks sloshing from upraised cups. A woman in sky-blue lipstick barked orders near the bar, pointing at teenage bartenders who moved like machines, their eyes glazed and arms flailing to keep up. Ola moved quickly, weaving through the throng, her nut basket clutched like a shield.

A hand brushed her shoulders. "Hello, gorgeous. Dance with me." She kept walking. "When you carry the egg basket, you don't dance." The man laughed, loud, low, and confident. "The one who can't dance always blames the ground." She froze. That voice! She turned to see Sergeant Polo. He stood tall in his civilian clothes, barely disguising his arrogance. His eyes raked over her, slow and intimate.

"Put it down," he said, nodding at the basket. "I'll guard it. Trust me, you'll remember this dance till your dying day."

"I came to sell nuts, not shake my behind."

"A cockroach in a henhouse doesn't cry innocence. Come on, beauty, stomp the ground before it swallows us whole."

Her throat dried.

Panic flickered through her mind.

She let the basket fall.

It hit the floor with a dull thud. The nuts scattered.

The gun clinked.

Someone screamed, "Gun!"

The bar erupted.

Patrons scattered in a frenzy. Bottles smashed. Chairs toppled. The music died with a shriek. Ola lunged for the weapon, her heart crashing in her chest.

Polo was faster.

His boot slammed down, sending the gun skidding across the floor with a clatter.

Ola turned to run, but the crowd was against her, bodies pushing, dragging, and chaos swallowing her whole.

A hand grabbed her wrist. Another clamped her arm. Then, cold steel shackled her.

"Got you," Polo hissed, yanking her backward. "You mad woman. We meet again."

She didn't resist. Not yet.

"Let's see what secrets your crafty head is hiding."

The slap came fast, snapping her head to the side. Then another. Her ears rang. Her lips bled.

He kicked her ribs. She collapsed.

Still, she remained silent.

Her silence only enraged him more. He dragged her to the police station to file a complaint.

The station reeked of sweat and mildew. The air hung thick with desperation. An officer looked up from a cracked desk as Polo dragged the woman in.

"Take her details," Polo barked, collapsing into a chair.

She still said nothing.

The young officer stammered as he flipped through the forms. Frustration tightened his face.

Polo picked up a baton.

"She doesn't want to talk?"

The first blow struck her spine. Then another. Her knees buckled.

Still, no sound escaped her lips.

"Put her in the storage room," he snapped. "Cells are full."

They dragged her down a narrow corridor. The cement walls were peeling and damp. Inmates hooted and jeered from rusted bars. Some laughed. One mimicked gunshots with his mouth. The officer then unlocked the rusted door. Darkness spilled out. He shoved her in. It was windowless, damp, and airless. A pail sat in the corner like a joke. The walls were too smooth to climb. The door shut behind her with the finality of a coffin lid. But she did not cry. She crouched in the dark and listened. Voices drifted from behind the walls.

"That's the mad woman from this morning."

"She had a gun."

"Must be military."

"She's no nuts vendor," Polo's voice cut in. "She's NFP. Tomorrow, I'll hand her over. The military will make her sing."

Her breath caught as hours passed. The cold seeped into her bones as she stood in the cell. Her muscles cramped. Her mind raced. At three o'clock in the morning, there was a sound. The click of a lock. Footsteps. Whispers.

CHAPTER FOURTEEN

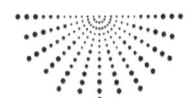

The darkness pressed against her skin like a wet cloth, thick with the stench of rust, sweat, and dried blood. Time had dissolved in the windowless cell, and hours were now folding into a single suffocating mass. Ola lay curled on the concrete slab, her breath shallow and her body aching from stillness. The silence was absolute until it broke.

A faint click.

Ola's eyes snapped open. Her heart stilled. She sat beside the wall and let her body sag as if in a deep sleep. The lock rattled again. A sliver of harsh light spilled into the cell.

Footsteps.

A torch beam crept across the floor, hovered, then fixed on her motionless figure. Two silhouettes shifted in the doorway and whispered.

"Think she's asleep?"

The voice was low and uncertain.

"Wake her up," came the rasp.

Still pretending to sleep, she felt the beam sting her eyelids. Her pulse remained steady. One . . . two . . . on the third command, an officer named Geo stormed in and grabbed her shoulder, giving it a rough shake. Ola blinked rapidly as the flashlight seared her vision. She slowly rose, her hands obedient, eyes wide, and adjusting.

"Well, well. The lady devil herself," Geo sneered, tilting his head in disdain. "You a rebel?"

"Speak!" barked Officer Peko, stepping closer, baton drawn. "Or we'll chop you into bits and feed you to the hounds!"

Their threats barely landed. Ola's mind raced, gears turning fast, scouring the cell for an opening.

"Deaf, are you?" Geo growled. "Let's fix that." He raised his baton.

A whisper of movement. Ola's foot swept under him. Geo's legs vanished from under him, his skull cracking against the floor with a sickening thud as he fell.

Peko lunged. Ola's back kick struck his hip. He howled and stumbled.

Geo groaned and rolled over. He pushed up, but her fist was already moving. The uppercut met his jaw with a pop, and his teeth snapped together. Blood sprayed as he bit his tongue.

She spun.

Peko's eyes widened just before her boot hit him on the side of the head. He crumpled. His gun clattered.

She pounced. Her fingers wrapped around the AK-47's grip just as Geo, dazed but furious, staggered behind her. He swung wildly.

Wrong move.

Ola ducked, then lifted him, yes, lifted him, and hurled his weight across the room. He slammed against the wall. The impact echoed like gunfire. He slumped, dazed until her foot crashed into his ribcage. A wheeze. Another kick. A scream. She dealt a final blow to his face. His front teeth scattered like rice. Blood pooled on his lips.

"M-my . . . teeth. . . ." he whimpered.

Ola adjusted the AK's strap and strode toward the door. Then she paused. A fire stirred inside her.

No. Not yet.

She turned back. A feral rage surged.

A storm of kicks rained on Geo and Peko's bodies, swift and punishing, aimed low, brutal, and biological. They groaned like broken things. She stepped back, spat on their mangled faces, and turned on her heels.

In the corridor, the jail erupted. Fists pounded the steel doors. "Set us free!" they screamed. Kobole dialects rose in a frantic chorus.

Ola slowed down and hesitated.

She stared at the cells, their faces pressed against the bars, desperate.

Her grip on the rifle was firm.

Not this time.

She moved on without a word.

They cursed behind her. Let them. She had seen what happened when the wrong crowd was freed. Nightlife had taught her that.

Then, gleam on metal.

Against the wall rested a military rifle with a coiled belt of bullets draped beside it, like a serpent ready to strike. Her eyes widened. "Hello, beauty," she whispered. She swapped the AK for the new beast and slung the belt over her shoulder.

Outside.

A bullet whizzed by, slicing through the air near her ear.

She dropped instantly, belly to the concrete, eyes scanning. She rolled, aimed, and fired.

The security lights shattered. Darkness swallowed everything.

In the fading glow of the station, she spotted a limping silhouette. She squeezed the trigger. The figure collapsed, writhing.

No time.

She bolted. Bullets chased her down the alleys. Screams echoed across the town. Dogs barked. Whistles pierced the air. Chaos.

She veered off the road and dove into a bush.

"She's there! There!" A woman's shrill voice exposed her.

Damn.

Her lungs screamed. Her legs burned. But she did not stop. Shouts, howls, and gunshots were behind her. But too close. She ran harder.

Don't think. Just move.

Eventually, she paused, hidden deep in green shadows. Her chest heaved. She yanked off the sweat-soaked wig and unfurled a map from her pouch. Her fingers traced the lines in the dim moonlight.

Still on route. The traps, yes, the traps were close.

She folded the map, breathed, and moved, quieter now and more focused.

Fifteen minutes.

Barking behind her. The police dogs had found where she had stopped. She glanced at her compass. Closer. Almost there.

Then she saw the final trap: a pit, spiked and laced with poison, camouflaged beneath the grass. She adjusted it, checked the rigging, then backed into the bushes. She covered herself with leaves and vanished into the forest floor.

Minutes passed. The jungle vibrated with the sound of approaching voices.

"She went this way."

"Her footprints are fresh!"

"Careful," Polo barked. "She's armed and dangerous. Move with caution. Civilians, go back! The forest belongs to the trained."

Murmurs. Complaints. Then, silence fell as the crowd thinned.

"Private Geo leads the dog unit!" Polo commanded. "Shoot to kill."

Geo snarled. "Go, babies. Tear the bitch apart!"

Bitch?

Ola's lips curled.

The dogs exploded forward, snarling, snapping, and with wild eyes.

A sense of fear prickled her scalp as they came into view. The dogs were massive and monstrous, with dripping muzzles.

They vanished down the trail.

Then . . . howling and whining.

Silence.

Geo shouted their names. No answer.

He sprinted ahead.

Seconds later. . . .

"Help! Oh, God!"

Ola smirked. "Who's the bitch now?"

By the time his squad arrived, Geo was impaled beside his precious dogs, lifeless on venom-dipped spikes. One young officer vomited and ran for the trees.

Too late.

Ola emerged behind him like a whisper, clamped a hand over his mouth, and slid a blade across his throat. He struggled, and then he didn't.

She eased him down. His weight settled silently in the underbrush. She reset the trap and retied the rope with practiced fingers. Then, she climbed swiftly and silently, vanishing into the canopy. She became part of the forest from her perch: a breath held in the leaves, a stillness sharpened by purpose. Below, twigs snapped. Movement. She climbed down, ready to flee.

"Stop!"

Polo's voice cracked like a whip through the trees. Ola froze mid-stride. Her boots sank into damp mulch. A shadow twitched in the tangled branches. It was Polo, puffing, panting, clutching his rifle like a child holding a lie. He had the high ground, but fear soaked his voice.

She tilted her head, her eyes narrowing as she met his gaze. Her fingers brushed the holster at her hip. One clean shot. Right between the eyes. But she hesitated. A bird scattered in the thicket behind her, startled by the chaos. Had the Kobole military heard the scuffle? She couldn't be sure.

Instead of firing, she smiled and winked with the sharp, wicked curve of her lips.

Then she vanished. The undergrowth closed around her like a secret. Polo erupted from the trees.

"You can kill us, but you won't kill our spirit, you mischief-makers!" His voice was hoarse with rage, echoing through the trees. "Tomorrow, the military and I are coming for you. You've opened a box of worms, Miss Smiley, and they will feast on your rotting corpse! Mark my words!" He kept screaming into the void, but Ola was long gone. His words trailed behind her like dry leaves in the wind.

She did not stop until dusk. At the edge of the rebel camp, her silhouette emerged through the trees, mud-spattered, breath heaving, eyes wide with urgency. The fighters snapped to attention. Conversations died mid-sentence. Even the forest seemed to still.

Within minutes, Mokote summoned them all. The fire hadn't been lit yet, but every soul gathered under the dusk canvas. Ola stood in their midst, trembling with exhaustion. Her words spilled, rapid-fire, strung together with panic and defiance. By the time she finished, even the youngest recruits sat stone-still, fear etched deep into their brows.

Mokote rose slowly. "No panic," he said. His voice was calm, but his eyes flicked toward the weapons stash. "Pack only what you need. We leave by nightfall."

No one argued. They moved with the silence of hunted animals. Blankets rolled. Cans stashed. Maps folded. Years in the forest had left them cluttered with scraps, metal trinkets, tattered journals, and charms from home. None of it mattered.

By 9:00 p.m., the camp was gone.

Shadows slipped south toward Kiri, a rebel-held territory in

Kobole. The forest swallowed their trail. But not their fear. Not their fires.

CHAPTER FIFTEEN

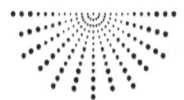

Their journey carved battle lines into their bodies, leaving scars from machetes and memories, bruises from bullets and betrayal. The Simba Battalion limped into Kiri with sunken eyes and weather-worn boots, their banner of survival clinging to the dust like a stubborn shadow. Twenty-three months and thirty days of war had stripped them of many things—men, certainty, sleep—but not Ola.

Mokote, once the lion's roar of the battalion, hadn't fallen to bullets but to the quiet cruelty of fever. Malaria had done what enemy fire could not. In his absence, the mantle of command passed, not by vote, but by gravity to Ola, the daughter of Odu.

She led with a blacksmith's fire and a midwife's mercy. Soldiers called her many things: mother, hammer, shield, judge. She stitched broken spirits with her silent presence and tore down arrogance with a single glance. She did not raise her voice; she raised standards. Those who knew her did not speak her name lightly. Ola was not just a leader; she was the flame in the hearth, the spine in the march, the silence before the storm.

By the time they reached Kiri's dusty hem, she had spoken to the southern rebels only through the crackle of wireless dispatches. No horns were needed to announce their arrival. A welcoming party stood waiting beneath the jacaranda trees, rifles slung and eyes sharp.

At their head stood a man—no, not a man. A marvel.

Ola's breath hitched.

The moment their eyes locked, something ancient stirred within her. The world, for a moment, forgot to spin. Heat coiled low in her belly, as though her veins had remembered fire. Her fingers, thick with calluses from months of combat, felt oddly foreign as she reached out to shake this royal Adonis' hand.

His grip was firm, not aggressive, but measured. And his eyes lingered on her, not in defiance or flirtation, but in wonder. As if he had just walked into a memory not yet made.

Ola felt her mouth move. Words tumbled out, guttural, automatic, but she would not have remembered them even if someone had written it down. Her hand lingered longer than decorum allowed, and when she finally let go, her fingers were reluctant to part from his.

He smiled, not with his lips, but with something deeper. Something behind the gaze. Ola pretended not to notice the heat rising in her cheeks. She pretended not to hear the hush among her soldiers. She pretended her heart had not just disobeyed a direct order.

Marko. That was the name someone mentioned.

She did not know then that the battlefield would not be the only terrain she would be asked to survive. Not with Marko in it.

As the two commanders stood beneath the jacaranda's shade, her gaze sharp as a blade, his softer than a lullaby, something unspoken, irretrievable, and irreversible bloomed quietly between them.

In the middle of a war, love does not ask for permission.

It simply arrives.

Things moved fast. Later that night, under a star-punched sky, the camp lay still, only the occasional cough or rustle of a shifting sentry disturbed the silence. In the command tent, a hurricane lantern cast soft golden halos dancing on canvas walls. Maps sprawled across the table, but neither Ola nor Marko looked at them. She sat cross-legged, her rifle propped beside her like a silent guardian. He leaned back on one elbow, close enough for their knees to touch. The air between them pulsed, not with words, but with the heavy silence of recognition.

"You don't speak much," he said at last, his voice a whisper, as though anything louder might break the fragile moment.

"War has a way of silencing things," she murmured.

He nodded. "But some silences speak."

She looked at him then, not as a commander weighing a comrade, but as a woman allowed, just for once, to be more than steel. His gaze did not devour her; it held her, like one might cradle something sacred. Slowly, as if resisting orders from their bodies, their fingers brushed across the map between them. A touch that lingered. Not urgent. Just real.

Ola's breath caught again. But this time, she did not pretend. She let it show. She let herself be seen.

Marko moved closer, until the scent of woodsmoke and leather filled her lungs. His hand cupped her cheek with a reverence she had never been offered, not even by peace. When he kissed her, it was not desperate. It wasn't even lust. It was an offering. A promise made in the language of touch, written on battle-worn skin. In that kiss, there were no ranks, rifles, or rebels—only two souls who, after losing everything, found each other.

For one night, Ola was no longer the commander. She was not legend. She was simply . . . loved.

Time did not gallop in Kobole. It crawled, bled, and learned to walk again. Seasons passed in grit and gunpowder. Ola and Marko were never seen apart, sometimes ducking beneath mortar smoke, sometimes poring over crumpled maps lit by the trembling glow of kerosene lamps. Their love was neither loud nor flowery. It was forged in fire. In quiet glances before battle, hands clasped beneath the moon, promises made with eyes because words were too fragile for the front lines.

Then came the turning tide.

Her eyes were sharp as the spear tips. Ola led the final charge herself, through the razor forests of Mutambo, across the salt-stained bunkers of the capital. She moved like a storm, disciplined, unyielding–not chasing vengeance, but the freedom whispered by her ancestors.

The palace fell before sunrise. Smoke curled like incense

over the ruins of the old regime. From its ashes, the flag of a new Kobole was rose, stitched by rebels and dreamers, soaked in the sweat of the broken, flapping like a heartbeat above the battered capital.

At the foot of the toppled statue of Dictator Boni, amid rubble and bullet casings, stood a man wrapped in white linen, dusty and blinking at the sky as if it were the first light he'd seen in years.

Father Angelo.

Once a captive of the New Freedom Pact rebels and later a prisoner of the collapsing regime, the Italian priest stood witness to a new era's birth. His once-white cassock was stained and threadbare. A tattered rosary still wrapped his wrist like a relic of survival. Tears shimmered in his eyes, not from fear but relief and reverence.

During the chaos of the final siege, Nunu had stumbled upon him, half-starved, barely conscious, as the charge he led broke open the prison cell. As the smoke cleared and hope flickered into flame, Nunu brought the priest forward, his heart pounding with joy. He led him straight to Ola, eager to share the miracle, that even in the rubble, something sacred had survived.

The priest approached, not to judge, but to bear witness not to insurgents, but to the architects of a fragile, hard-won peace. Ola stepped forward, sweat still dripping from her brow, her hands scraped raw from battle. He smiled through cracked lips and placed a trembling hand over her heart.

"You led them, child," he whispered. "You turned warriors into a nation."

Tears. She nodded.

Before she could speak, Marko appeared behind her, draping a simple shawl over her shoulders. No crown. No medals. Just the cloth of a people finally at rest.

Ola clasped Marko's hand and nodded to the priest. The three stood still, heat rising from scorched earth, ash swirling like memory. Her eyes, sharp as ever, did not waver from the horizon. Love had not loosened her grip; it had only tempered her resolve.

The gunfire had quieted and the slogans faded, but something deeper pulsed beneath the soil. With her shoulders squared and chin lifted, she stepped forward, her bare feet brushing against the broken ground, not seeking comfort but carving a path. Marko moved beside her, his breath steady. Father Angelo trailed behind, rosary whispering with each step. No more chants. No more drums. Only the quiet thrum of a nation waking, watching Ola, its lioness, walk into the bones of a future she helped shape.

CHAPTER SIXTEEN

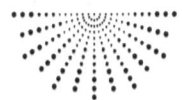

The midday sun scorched Nyungu village, casting long shadows beneath thatched roofs and parched mango trees. Chickens scattered as dust danced in the air, carrying whispers of the strange. A tremor rose from the earth, not an earthquake, but something more terrifying and alive.

Children ran barefoot, eyes wide with wonder. Women clutched their headscarves tighter. A sharp cry rang out from the watch hill. The herd boys dropped their sticks and ran. Market women froze mid-bargain. Even the cattle lifted their heads in response.

"Trucks! Soldiers, soldiers are coming!"

Somewhere beyond the low hills, a convoy of green-painted military trucks tore through the sleeping savannah, rattling the dry silence with every revolution of their tires.

Within minutes, the village square descended into chaos. Men dropped hoes mid-swing, mothers called out frantically for their children, and the old healer bolted his hut, forgetting his divination bones.

From the northern bend, a column of matte-green army trucks rolled forward, a dozen in number, each bearing the insignia of the NFP, the very force that had toppled the iron-fisted regime. Blue and gold flags fluttered in the wind, fierce and new. The soldiers stood stiff and silent, faces unreadable behind dark glasses. The villagers stood torn between fear and celebration.

Chief Odu stood trembling beneath the baobab tree, staff in hand, breath shallow. Soldiers? For him? He had only finished arguing with Ayami, who had burst into the house, babbling nonsense about the new president being their daughter. Their daughter. He'd laughed her off. Crazy radio. Crazier still were the Ayamis who believe it.

Now, the rumble of war trucks crushed the air.

The lead vehicle stopped abruptly, its engine still purring. Doors swung open. Then, from within, stepped Nunu. Taller now. Shoulders broad as a warrior's. He wore a crisp NFP ceremonial uniform with a golden sash across his chest.

Nunu descended, and the crowd drew back as though a spirit had landed.

"Father," he called, loud enough to pierce the thick tension, "by order of the President of the Republic of Kobole, daughter of Odu, you and our mother are summoned to the capital. Your presence is requested at her inauguration as President of Kobole."

The square fell silent. Even the chickens stopped scratching.

Chief Odu's staff slipped from his hand and clattered to the ground. "What . . . did you say?"

Gasps swept through the crowd like wildfire. The whispers started:

"The President?"

"Ola? Our Ola?"

"She ran away!"

"She defied the blade!"

Someone dropped to their knees and began to shout praises. Then came the stampede.

Children screamed, not from fear, but from joy. Young men surged forward for a glimpse of Nunu. Women danced in place, ululating with hands flung skyward. Elders were swept along like dry leaves in a storm of celebration. A boy climbed a tree and yelled, "Ola is the President! Nyungu blood rules Kobole!"

But not all was joy.

Some villagers stumbled back, torn between pride and guilt. The girl they shunned, the one they had once called cursed for fleeing the ritual, had returned, crowned by revolution. Their shame echoed louder than the drums that now thundered across the homesteads.

Chief Odu did not speak. His lips moved, but no words came. Ayami, tears streaming down her face, broke through the crowd and reached for Nunu. She embraced her son as if he were Ola.

"My baby girl. . . ." she whispered. "She still remembers us."

Behind them, soldiers gently created space, forming a protective circle as the presidential car crept forward.

Chief Odu finally found his voice. "She . . . she wants me there? After all I said? After all I. . . ."

Nunu nodded solemnly. "She said no nation can heal without its roots present."

Tears welled in Odu's eyes. He straightened his robe with his shaking hands.

"Then let the roots rise."

Chief Odu stood in the middle of his hut like a goat caught in a rainstorm: arms stiff, eyes wild, and trousers halfway up his thighs.

"These devil's skins are trying to eat me!" he barked, hopping on one leg as the fabric clung to his knees like angry bees. "Ayami! Are you sure this is how city men wear them?"

His wife stifled a laugh behind her hands. "Pull them up, Odu. Not sideways."

He yanked again. The trousers finally shot up his legs with a violent snap that made him yelp in pain. His wide hips groaned against the strange fabric. "A man could suffocate in these! My goats wouldn't forgive me if I died dressed like a church bell."

Then came the shoes.

Chief Odu stared at the polished black monstrosities, like snake skins enchanted by dark sorcery. "These are too small. My feet are warriors, not river fish!"

"You must wear them, not argue with them," Ayami replied, biting her lips to hold back laughter.

After much stomping, twisting, and one loud fart, the shoes were finally on, though his toes stuck out like mutinous prisoners. He tried to walk but waddled like a duck on hot porridge, pausing every few steps to grimace and curse the inventor of "tight foot coffins."

"I'm dressed like a foreign bridegroom going to marry his

confusion," he grumbled, adjusting his ill-fitting shirt awkwardly tucked into his trousers. "I have never worn trousers in all my days. And now my buttocks feel ambushed!"

Ayami stepped back and examined him with loving mischief. "You look . . . presidential, Odu."

He squinted suspiciously. "Are you mocking me, woman?"

"Never," she said, slipping a ceremonial beaded necklace over his head. "You are going to meet the President. You must look the part."

He sighed, puffed out his chest, and limped toward the door, wobbling like a proud, broken-legged rooster.

"Let the country tremble," he muttered as he walked to the waiting car. "Chief Odu walks in shoes today."

The village lined up to watch the great Chief of Nyungu take his first painful, hilarious steps into history. As the convoy turned back toward the capital, drums followed them, laughter chased their wheels, and behind them, Nyungu erupted in a storm of regret, redemption, and revolution.

Ola, daughter of Odu, had returned, not as a runaway girl, but as the lioness queen of a new nation. The drums thundered as the motorcade rolled past the cheering crowds, their ululations slicing through the morning air like arrows of joy.

CHAPTER SEVENTEEN

By the time they reached the city, banners with Ola's face fluttered across buildings, a storm of hope sweeping through Kobole. A sleek black car purred to a stop at the grand palace gates beneath the national flag, rising against the sun. The door opened. Chief Odu stepped out like a confused tortoise. His feet, crammed into shiny shoes, moved slowly, each step a battle between his ancestral dignity and modern discomfort. His once-commanding frame sagged awkwardly in a borrowed suit, and he kept tugging at his trousers, as though they might betray him publicly.

Beside him, Ayami walked with her head held high, wrapped in a richly woven sash. Her eyes scanning the palace she had never imagined entering without kneeling.

Odu swallowed hard. The red carpet stretched like a river of judgment.

And then he saw her.

Ola stood at the top of the marble steps, clad in crimson silk embroidered with golden thread that snaked over her shoulders. The presidential sash kissed her collarbones. Her gaze locked on his, steady and unreadable. A braided crown shimmered in the sunlight. Beside her stood Marko, tall, poised, and devastatingly handsome, like a general carved from onyx. But it was Ola's eyes that froze Odu in place.

A lump rose in his throat.

"I thought they were lying," he whispered to Ayami in disbelief. "But that is her. That is *my daughter*."

Ola descended, one step then another. Her heels clicked against the marble, slow and deliberate like a war drum. The cheering crowd quieted. The air thickened.

Chief Odu, once the roaring lion of Nyungu, dropped to his knees.

"My daughter," he rasped, his voice breaking. "Forgive the blindness of your father. I threw you into the wind . . . but the wind returned you as a storm."

Ola paused, inches from him.

A heartbeat passed, everything was still. Then she knelt. She gently took his weathered hands in hers. When she spoke, her voice trembled with fire and grace.

"I never left you, Baba. You turned your back, but I walked forward. For both of us."

She turned to Ayami, hugging her tightly, kissing her cheeks as the old woman clung to her and wept.

Tears rolled down Odu's face, carving silent rivers through the dust of his years.

The crowd erupted. Some wept, others clapped, and many raised their fists in solidarity.

"Baba," Ola said, smiling through tears, "I want you to meet an old friend."

"Who is that one, my lost and found daughter?" Odu asked, still breathless.

From behind the ceremonial guards, Fr. Angello appeared. Odu burst into tears once again, reaching for him like a brother long dead and returned from the grave.

From the palace balcony, Marko stood still, a quiet sentinel above the roaring crowd. One hand rested over his heart. His gaze never left her: Ola, daughter of Odu, commander of Simba, the woman who had once defied a knife and now knelt in forgiveness before the man who had cast her away.

In that moment, she was not only his beloved. She was history rethreading its fabric, pain blooming into power, rejection bending into reconciliation. She was the heartbeat of a nation rising from ashes.

Tomorrow, the world would call her President.

Marko closed his eyes, letting the evening breeze wash over him, thick with song, drumbeat and the scent of change. He had stood beside her through fire and exile, through backdoor strategy meetings, and battlefield silence. But this, this was something else. This was a greater achievement.

She had not just led Kobole into a new dawn. She was the dawn.

As the last sliver of sun melted into the horizon, the palace lights blinked on, bathing the city in a golden hush. Tomorrow was the inauguration day. And he, Marko the fighter, the lover, the witness, could not have been prouder of the woman walking into destiny with the strength of a storm and the tenderness of a home.

CHAPTER EIGHTEEN

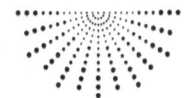

The city of Kobole had never breathed like this before. At the cusp of dawn, the capital stirred, not with grogginess but with electric anticipation. The air smelled of roasted groundnuts, fresh dew, and the faint tang of marula wine spilled in joyous haste. Sunlight unfurled across the city like a royal mat, catching the glittering beadwork and bronze bangles of dancers already moving in rhythm. The streets pulsed with color, bold streaks of kente, kikoi, barkcloth, and ankara rippling in the breeze, each thread whispering ancestral tales. Ribbons fluttered like tongues from balconies and roadside stalls, speaking in celebration.

Children, cheeks painted in red ochre and gold, bore Ola's insignia, a rising sun cupped by open hands—on their foreheads, chests, and even bare backs. The scent of woodsmoke and sweat mingled with the floral sweetness of crushed hibiscus petals scattered into the crowd. Elders sat like sentinels in woven palm-frond chairs, hands weathered but steady, clapping in a slow, sacred rhythm, as if conjuring the spirit of a new era with each beat.

Outside the National Assembly Grounds, the crowd was a living river, shoulder to shoulder, breath by breath. Former rebels with machete scars stood beside cattle herders in dust-stained cloaks. Market women with babies tied to their backs chanted next to university scholars in tweed and cowrie neck-laces. Priests sprinkled holy water while barefoot children darted between their legs, laughing like flutes. Draped in cere-monial silks, foreign dignitaries looked on with awe as one hundred drums began to speak. Their rhythm was thunderous, syncopated, primal, shaking dust from the bones of the earth and calling up ancestors from forgotten graves.

And then, the horns. Not metallic blasts of conquest, but ancient, breathy, rounded sounds, a sound that stirred memory.

The gates creaked . . . then flung open.

She came.

Ola, Daughter of Odu and Granddaughter of Ode.

Her robe flowed like a river of resistance, stitched from rebel banners, dyed with indigo and ash, embroidered with sacred emblems from all sixty-five tribes. Each step whispered defiance and promise. Her braids were coiled high, thick, and regal, crowned with coral and lion teeth, each earned through struggle. Gold cuffs caught the sun on her wrists, but it was her eyes that commanded: wide, dark, heavy with sorrow, aflame with justice. Eyes that had seen comrades buried nameless, chil-dren silenced, futures orphaned.

Marko walked beside her, silent and rooted. In his black agbada rimmed with blood-red thread, he was both warrior and mourner. His hand hovered behind hers, never leading, never needing to. Just there. Steady. Always.

Ola climbed the marble steps. The crowd swelled with her ascent. Cheers thundered. Ululations pierced the air like birdsong. Some wept. Some sang. Some dropped to their knees and kissed the earth. The trembling was not fear; it was joy so deep it cracked the soil open.

She raised one fist. A thousand followed.

Unity. Defiance. Rebirth.

The old dictator's banner sagged, then slipped down the pole like a dying breath. In its place, a new flag was unfurled:

Green for the land.

Gold for the sun.

Red for the blood that bought this day.

A barefoot child, eyes wide, skin still glazed with the war's shadows, carried the presidential sash forward on a velvet cushion. Green and gold. Heavy not just with thread, but with memory.

Ola knelt.

"For every child who thought they were forgotten," she whispered, her voice low and trembling like a prayer.

Then she rose, tall as history, and faced the nation.

"I, Ola, daughter of Odu, child of Nyungu, servant of the people, do solemnly swear. . . ."

After taking her oath, the Nyungu lioness, now the President of Kobole, let her voice ring out. Not in policy. Not in platitudes. But in promise.

She said, "The Chief Justice of our Supreme Court, dignitaries from Kobole and beyond, cultural leaders, my beloved parents, fellow citizens, ladies and gentlemen, all protocols observed. . . .

"My name is Ola, and I am the daughter of Chief Odu from the Nyungu community. I stand before you today not because of my merit alone, but because of the mysterious hand of fate. Years ago, I was a frightened girl, fleeing one culture's blade into the unknown. Born in pain, that journey led me here as your President, and still, as your daughter.

"In the silence of the bush, between raids and resistance, I would spare moments to read books smuggled from the rebel base. These books nourished my mind while I nursed my wounds. In those pages, I met voices from distant lands, and our own, echoing timeless truths. And today, I wish to share some of those beautiful ideas with you.

"Let me begin by honoring our African values. We were taught to be communal, humane, spiritually grounded, and accountable to one another. Our elders raised us with wisdom, courage, and restraint. However, let us also remember that colonization did not just take our land. It rewrote our minds. As Frantz Fanon taught us, 'Colonialism is not satisfied merely with holding a people in its grip . . . it distorts, disfigures and destroys.' It labeled our gods as primitive, our customs as savage, and our languages as inferior.

"Ngũgĩ wa Thiong'o reminds us that 'colonialism begins with language.' Therefore, today, we reclaim our story, not by rejecting all that is foreign but by recentering what is authentically ours. We must distinguish between heritage and harm. We must revisit customs like female genital mutilation, child marriage, and bride inheritance, not with blind loyalty, but with courage. Tradition should not be a cage. It must be a compass. Culture evolves. We must evolve with it without apology.

"Let us now speak of emancipation. Africa's future cannot be built on the backs of silenced women. Progress demands that girls sit in classrooms, lead in boardrooms, and govern in parliaments. But emancipation is not only for the girl child. We must raise our boys, too. Raise them to value consent, to practice empathy, to see strength not in domination, but in justice. When we educate one gender and neglect the other, we build a lopsided society. 'Each generation must, out of relative obscurity, discover its mission, fulfill it or betray it,' Fanon warned. This is our mission. If we raise lions and doves in the same cage and expect peace, we fool no one but ourselves.

"Education must now lead to liberation, not merely memorization, but awakening. Not only Western textbooks but also African wisdom. Before colonial schools, the village was the classroom. Every elder was a teacher. Every experience was a lesson. Beneath the trees, beside the fires, in the rhythm of the drum and the hush of the hunt, knowledge was alive, rooted, shared, and inseparable from life. We must revive that spirit of *Ubuntu:* 'A person is a person through other persons', often paraphrased as 'I am because you are'.

"Ubuntu is not a slogan. It is a philosophy of mutual becoming. It teaches that our humanity is intertwined, that dignity cannot be individual if it is not shared. Education, therefore, must connect, not isolate. It must remind every child that learning is not a race to the top, but a walk alongside others. That brilliance is found not in answers, but in the humility to ask the right questions.

"Let us build classrooms that feel like the hearth and the

courtyard. Let the curriculum sing in proverbs, be measured in harvests, and be tested not only by exams but by how much a student uplifts their community. Let us restore pride in black-smithing, weaving, music, storytelling, farming, and healing. Not as relics of the past, but as technologies of culture, as knowledge systems that endured not because they were primitive, but because they were wise.

"In this age of machines, let us not forget the hand. In this era of algorithms, let us not discard the elder. In Africa, when an elder dies, it is as if a whole library has burned to the ground. Their wisdom, stories, and lived truths not stored in cloud servers, but in memory, language, and presence. Every society that forgets its roots eventually forgets its soul. Kobole, and Africa at large, must never lose hers again.

"Ngũgĩ wa Thiong'o warned us: 'The bullet was the means of physical subjugation. Language was the means of the spiritual subjugation.' We must therefore decolonize our curriculum. English, French, and other foreign tongues should not be the only passports to opportunity. Yet across Kobole and much of Africa, millions of Indigenous children begin school in a foreign language. This practice silences them from day one and turns them into strangers in their own skin. As Chinweizu described, this is 'mental slavery in a school uniform.' It is not merely misguided, it is a polite bureaucratic crime.

"I do not believe this is an accident. It is the lingering architecture of colonial education, that elevated foreign knowledge while erasing Indigenous identity. Amílcar Cabral reminded us that 'To exist is to resist.' Our ways of knowing matter. Intelligence wears many faces; some write essays, others carve wood, grow food, or birth songs.

"Education must become our spear and our shield. Not only in books from Oxford and Paris, but also in the wisdom carried in our songs, in the calloused hands of blacksmiths, the careful fingers of weavers, and in the healing roots known only to our grandmothers. Before Africa had chalkboard, the forest was our blackboard, and the moon our lamp.

"We must also end the alienation of our youth. Too many are trained to escape, not to lead. They speak like Londoners but feel lost in their own villages. Fanon called it 'black skin, white masks.' This is how we lose our doctors and innovators to distant lands. Our schools must nurture belonging, not just ambition.

"And yes, we must bridge the 'technical now' versus 'technical know-how.' We boast engineers who have never held a wrench, economists who have never planted a seed, and planners who have never walked the dusty roads of the communities they serve. Let us stop worshipping titles and start honoring practical competence.

"Colonial education shifted us from practice to theory, from the field to the chalkboard, from action to abstraction. It turned the African child into a passive listener, an empty tin to be filled by the all-knowing teacher. As Paulo Freire warned, 'Education thus becomes an act of depositing, in which the students are the depositories and the teacher is the depositor . . . an act of banking, not knowing.' This so-called 'banking model' has no room for critical thinking, creativity, or context. It disconnects learning from living.

"Cabral challenged us to 'return to the source.' That source is not abstraction, it is applied knowledge rooted in reality. It is the farmer who understands the seasons, the midwife who knows the rhythms of life, the artisan who solves with their hands what no formula can predict. We must rebuild an education system that balances theory with craft, the mind with the hand, and knowledge with usefulness.

"Education holds a double edge: it can enslave the mind or set it free. Kobole and African scholars must reclaim what was stolen, challenging not only the remnants of colonial systems but also the leaders who keep them alive.

"But my people, let us not deceive ourselves, no amount of learning or culture can save us if we do not confront the cancer of corruption and dictatorship. What is the worth of a degree when jobs are sold to the highest bidder? What is the use of a vote when leaders rule by fear? What dignity remains when national budgets disappear while hospitals crumble and citizens starve?

"We must be clear: corruption is not a culture. Silence is not peace. Fear is not governance. Fanon warned us that postcolonial elites often mimic colonial power, becoming 'a transmission line between the metropolitan capital and the colony.' True leadership serves the people, not the self, not the clan, not the tribe, and not foreign masters. As your President, I vow this: I will not be a ruler. I will be a servant of all.

"Let us not forget that Kobole is home to sixty-five tribes. I am of the Nyungu. However, my presidency is not for Nyungu alone. I lead as the daughter of all people. Diversity is not a weakness; it is our deepest wealth. The drumbeats of Kobole may sound different from village to village, but together, they can create a symphony. Even a stew needs many spices.

"To preserve that symphony, we must embrace the spirit of Ubuntu—I am because we are—and live by the principle of convivitribality: the peaceful and dignified coexistence of tribes. Our ancestors did not survive by silencing difference, but by respecting it. Ubuntu teaches us that *our* humanity is bound together. That your pain is mine, and your dignity is my own.

"But this dream of shared belonging is under siege. Tribalism has become a silent cancer. It is invisible in law but inscribed in daily life. In the West, racism divides skin; in Africa, tribalism divides kin. It whispers in job offers, festers in electoral alliances, poisons classrooms, and sometimes leads to genocide. We must name it. We must end it. Not in speeches alone, but in systems.

"No tribe should stand above another. No child should grow up believing that their language, lineage, or land makes them second-class. Unity must not mean uniformity, but solidarity. Let us teach our youth that to uplift one tribe while degrading another is not patriotism. It is sabotage. Let us build a Kobole, and an Africa, where every tribe has a voice but no tribe monopolizes the truth. Let the next generation inherit not old grudges, but shared purpose. Let every tribe bring its drum, its dance, its proverb to the fire, not to compete, but to contribute. Only then can we become not a nation of fragments, but a family of nations. Not by force, but by choice.

"At this pivotal moment, let us understand that unity alone will not save us if the land that feeds us dies. Without the rivers, there will be no song to carry. Without the forests, there will be no shade for our dreams. Climate change is no distant specter; it is the harsh reality shaping our every breath and tomorrow's fate. Our ancient forests, guardians of life, are vanishing. Our rivers, once veins of vitality, now choke beneath the weight of neglect. The air hangs heavy, thickened by smoke and sorrow.

Environmental justice is not a choice or luxury; it is an imperative for survival. As Thomas Sankara declared, 'You cannot carry out fundamental change without a certain amount of madness.' This madness must ignite within us the fearless resolve to defend and restore our sacred land.

"And finally, let us cast aside this begging-bowl mentality once and for all. Foreign aid may serve as a bridge, but it must never become a crutch that stifles our sovereignty. As Sankara thundered, 'He who feeds you, controls you.' We must break free from those chains. Molefi Kete Asante reminds us: 'No people can be truly free if they do not control their own narrative.' It is time for Kobole, for Africa, to reclaim our story. Not as fragments borrowed or stolen, but as architects of our destiny.

"Beneath our soil lies a treasure more precious than gold. The boundless wealth of our land and the unstoppable genius of our youth. This is the power to not merely survive, but to rise, to build, to thrive in a world that has too long doubted us.

"To transform Kobole, to transform Africa, we must first believe. Believe in ourselves, in our girls and boys, in our ancestors' roots, and in the earth that cradles us all. As Fanon declared, 'Each generation must discover its mission.' This is ours. This is our hour. The dawn awaits, and we shall be the storm that becomes the dawn.

"May we walk boldly into tomorrow, with wisdom in our hearts, justice in our hands, and the wind of change at our backs.

"Thank you for your attention."

As Ola stepped down from the podium, a wave of stunned silence enveloped the crowd, thick, reverent, and electric. It was as if the nation inhaled together, pausing at the precipice of history.

Subsequently, the ground erupted.

A sound swelled from the people, not mere noise but something primal, full-bodied, and ancestral. Sharp and layered, a thousand ululations spiraled into the sky, the women's voices shaking the clouds loose. The drums responded faster now, hands pounding hides with reckless joy. Calabashes rattled. Shakers sang. The rhythm leapt from foot to foot like wildfire across dry grass.

Children tossed marigold petals and ripped cassava leaves into the air, giggling as their laughter caught in the breeze. Young men flipped through the air, bare chests glistening with sweat, feet slamming the red earth. Old women, bones creaky but spirits blazing, broke into ceremonial dances, their backs swaying to songs they had not dared to sing aloud in years. From rooftops, balconies, and mango trees, voices soared: "Long live the Lioness! Long live Kobole!"

The clapping roared like rolling thunder. Feet stomped in unison. The men beat their walking sticks into the ground with joy. One woman fell to her knees, her arms raised to the heavens, tears cutting through the white ash on her face. "It is finished," she wept. "The old night has passed."

Singers emerged in clusters, voices blending in layered harmony, praising not just Ola but every soul who had walked through fire for this dawn. The air smelled of celebration, burning sage, roasted maize, sweat, dust, and the heady sweetness of mangoes cracked open and passed around by strangers who now felt like family.

A group of children lifted a banner, its rough brushstrokes

shouting: THE DUST HAS SETTLED. THE THUNDER HAS SPOKEN.

Above all, Kobole's new flag danced in the wind like a living thing, baptized not in ink but in song, sacrifice, and soil.

Long after the crowd had dispersed,
And the flags lay still from their dance,
A single truth remained
Not shouted, but etched in the hush.
It echoed through hills and valleys,
Wove through rivers once sworn to divide,
Crept into homes that had once trembled with fear,
And whispered beneath every thatched roof and stone:
Kobole had found its breath again.
Not in thunder alone, but in rising dust.
In memory. In fire. In name.
Her name was Ola,
Daughter of dust.
Daughter of thunder.
Bearer of the storm that became dawn.

THE END

NOTES

p. 105, "As Frantz Fanon taught us, 'Colonialism is not satisfied. . . .'"
Frantz Fanon, *The Wretched of the Earth*, trans. Richard Philcox (Grove Press, 2004), 210.

p. 105, "Ngũgĩ wa Thiong'o reminds us that 'colonialism begins with language.'"
Ngũgĩ wa Thiong'o, *Decolonising the Mind: The Politics of Language in African Literature* (East African Educational Publishers, 1986), 4.

p. 105, "Each generation must, out of relative obscurity, discover its mission, fulfill it or betray it, . . .'"
Fanon, *The Wretched*, 206.

p. 105, "We must revive that spirit of Ubuntu: 'A person is a person through other persons', . . .'"
Desmond Tutu, *No Future Without Forgiveness* (Doubleday, 1999), 31.

p. 106, "Ngũgĩ wa Thiong'o warned us: 'The bullet was the means of physical subjugation.'"
wa Thiong'o. *Decolonising the Mind*, 9.

p. 106, "As Chinweizu described, this is 'mental slavery in a school uniform.'"
Chinweizu, *The West and the Rest of Us: White Predators, Black Slavers and the African Elite* (Pero Press, 1975), 261.

p. 106, "Amílcar Cabral reminded us that 'To exist is to resist.'"
Amílcar Cabral. *Resistance and Decolonization*, ed. Carey Nelson, trans. Dan Wood (Monthly Review Press, 2016) 45.

p. 107, "Fanon called it 'black skin, white masks.'"
Frantz Fanon. *Black Skin, White Masks*, trans. Charles Lam Markmann (Grove Press, 1967).

p. 107, "As Paulo Freire warned, 'Education thus becomes an act of depositing, . . .'"
Paulo Freire, *Pedagogy of the Oppressed*, trans. Myra Bergman Ramos (Continuum, 1970) 72.

p. 107, "Cabral challenged us to 'return to the source.'"
Amílcar Cabral, *Return to the Source: Selected Speeches* (Monthly Review Press, 1973) 12.

p. 108, "Fanon warned us that postcolonial elites often mimic colonial power, . . .'"
Fanon, *The Wretched*, 152.

p. 109, "As Thomas Sankara declared, 'You cannot carry out fundamental change . . .'" and "As Sankara thundered, 'He who feeds you, controls you.'"
Thomas Sankara, *Thomas Sankara Speaks: The Burkina Faso Revolution 1983–87*, ed. Michel Prairie (Pathfinder Press, 2007) 233.

p. 109, "Molefi Kete Asante reminds us: 'No people can be truly free . . .'"
Molefi Kete Asante, *The Afrocentric Idea* (Temple University Press, 1998) 12.

p. 110, "As Fanon declared, 'Each generation must discover its mission.'"
Fanon, *The Wretched*, 210.

ACKNOWLEDGMENTS

My deepest gratitude to Miss **Lyndah Wasike** for her invaluable insights, **Mr Lutaaya Eric** for typing the manuscript, Mr **Sylvester Ochieng Juma** for his meticulous editing, and Mr **Robert Harrison** for his expert proofreading and formatting support. Your contributions shaped this work in profound ways.

ABOUT THE AUTHOR

Robert G. Mukasa is a Ugandan writer, educator, and researcher whose work bridges storytelling, culture, and social consciousness. Drawing from Africa's rich oral traditions and his deep understanding of education and community  life, Robert crafts narratives that explore resilience, resistance, and the human spirit in the face of cultural and political storms.

He holds a PhD in Curriculum and Instruction from Texas Tech University, where his research focused on teacher education, indigenous knowledge systems, and language in education. Beyond academia, Robert is passionate about using storytelling as a tool for reflection, liberation, and social change.

Daughter of Dust and Thunder is his latest work, a vivid and emotionally charged tale that captures the struggle for freedom and the enduring strength of the human heart.

Readers can connect with Robert G. Mukasa and learn more about his work through:

Website: https://sophiraeduconsultancy.com/
Email: sophiraeduconsultancy@gmail.com
YouTube: http://www.youtube.com/@sophirafireplace